of the C...

and their brave canine partners

Officer: Nina Atkins

K-9 Partner: Sam the rottweiler

Assignment: Team up with US Marshal Thomas Grant to track down a serial killer at Christmas.

Officer: Tim Ramsey

K-9 Partner: Frodo the German shepherd

Assignment: Find the arsonist Vickie Petrov saw in action and keep her alive to see the new year.

With over seventy books published and millions in print, **Lenora Worth** writes award-winning romance and romantic suspense. Three of her books finaled in the ACFW Carol Awards, and her Love Inspired Suspense novel *Body of Evidence* became a *New York Times* bestseller. Her novella in *Mistletoe Kisses* made her a *USA TODAY* bestselling author. Lenora goes on adventures with her retired husband, Don, and enjoys reading, baking and shopping...especially shoe shopping.

Terri Reed's romance and romantic suspense novels have appeared on the *Publishers Weekly* top twenty-five and Nielsen BookScan's top one hundred lists, and have been featured in *USA TODAY*, *Christian Fiction Magazine* and *RT Book Reviews*. Her books have been finalists for the Romance Writers of America RITA® Award and the National Readers' Choice Award, and finalists three times for the American Christian Fiction Writers Carol Award. Contact Terri at terrireed.com or PO Box 19555, Portland, OR 97224.

CLASSIFIED K-9 UNIT CHRISTMAS

LENORA WORTH
TERRI REED

(H) HARLEQUIN® LOVE INSPIRED® SUSPENSE

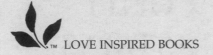 LOVE INSPIRED BOOKS

Recycling programs for this product may not exist in your area.

ISBN-13: 978-0-373-67863-1

Classified K-9 Unit Christmas

Copyright © 2017 by Harlequin Books S.A.

Special thanks and acknowledgment are given to Lenora Worth and Terri Reed for their contribution to the Classified K-9 Unit series.

The publisher acknowledges the copyright holders of the individual works as follows:

A Killer Christmas
Copyright © 2017 by Harlequin Books S.A.

Yuletide Stalking
Copyright © 2017 by Harlequin Books S.A.

www.Harlequin.com

Printed in U.S.A.

CONTENTS

A KILLER CHRISTMAS

Lenora Worth

To Terri Reed—you make me proud every day.
I'm so glad to be here with you!

For He will give His angels charge concerning you
to guard you in all of your ways.
–Psalms 91:11

ONE

The full moon grinned down on her with a wintry smile. FBI Tactical K-9 Unit Agent Nina Atkins held on to the leash and kept an eye on the big dog running with her. Sam loved being outside, no matter the weather, no matter the crunch of snow underneath his paws. The three-year-old K-9 rottweiler, a smart but gentle giant that specialized in cadaver detection, had no idea that most humans were terrified of him. Especially the criminal kind.

Tonight, however, they weren't looking for criminals. Nina was just out for a nice run and then home to a long, hot shower. Two weeks before Christmas, and after a harrowing year where one of their own had gone bad and lost his life, thankfully all was quiet around the Billings, Montana, FBI Tactical K-9 Unit headquarters. Special Agent in Charge Max West would be back before Christmas, but right now he was taking some time off with his bride, Katerina. Even tech wiz Dylan O'Leary had taken a few days away to spend some time with the parents of his wife, Zara. So many of her friends and fellow agents had fallen in love lately, Nina's head was spinning. Which was probably why she'd felt the need for a quick run. She lived for her work. No time for romance. Okay, maybe she'd just given up on a love life since her last brief relationship had fizzled out like a mountain stream in a serious drought.

Nina lived about twenty miles from downtown Billings, in the quaint town of Iris Rock. Regardless of her single status, she loved going on these nightly runs through the quiet foothills near the Elk Basin.

"C'mon, Sam," Nina said now, her nose cold. "Just around the bend and then we'll cool down on the way home."

Sam woofed in response, comfortable in his own rich brown fur. But instead of moving on, the big dog came to an abrupt halt that almost threw Nina right over his broad body.

"Sam?"

The rottweiler glanced back at her with his work expression. What kind of scent had he picked up?

Then she heard something.

"I don't know anything. Please, don't do this."

Female. Youngish voice. Scared and shaky.

Giving Sam a hand signal to stay quiet, Nina moved from the narrow gravel jogging path to the snow-covered woods, each footstep slow and calculated. Sam led the way, as quiet as a desert rat.

"I need the key. The senator said you'd give it to me."

Nina and Sam hid behind a copse of trees and dead brambles and watched the two figures a few yards away, standing in an open spot.

A big, tall man was holding a gun on a young woman with long dark hair. The girl was sobbing and wringing her hands out, palms up. Nina recognized that defensive move.

Was he going to shoot her?

Then Nina noticed something else.

A shallow, open pit right behind the girl. Could that be a newly dug grave?

Nina didn't stop to ponder that question, but she knew to be careful, too. Giving Sam another "quiet" signal, she called out, "Hey, everything okay here?"

The girl gasped and stared at her with fear-filled eyes, but stayed frozen to the spot.

The man turned to face her. Nina used a hand signal to allow Sam to bark, hoping to distract the man so the girl could run. The dog did his job, his ferocious bark echoing loudly out over the winter woods. Since she didn't have her weapon, Sam was Nina's only hope right now in stopping the girl from getting shot. That could give her time to call for help.

The man stared at Nina, giving her a good view of his face in the eerie white light from the moon. He shot at her and just missed, and then pivoted back toward the girl, weapon in hand. Sam kept barking. The man looked panicked, so Nina motioned the rottweiler forward, all the while taking in the assailant's appearance.

The big dog growled, but stopped when she signaled him. "My dog is trained to attack," she said. "You should drop that gun now."

The man shook his head and raised the gun, but Nina signaled Sam again. The animal danced and barked, causing a panicked expression on the man's face. He started backing away, but in a lightning-fast move, pivoted and took one quick shot at the girl.

She screamed, grabbed at her shoulder and fell into the open pit behind her as the gunman disappeared into the woods.

Sam kept barking, eager for some action.

Nina pulled out her phone and hurriedly called in the crime, describing the scene and her location. "Suspect somewhere in the Iris Rock woods just off the Eastern trail."

Jumping down into the pit, she breathed a sigh of relief. The girl was still alive, though her pulse was weak. Nina almost sent Sam after the man, but instead ordered him to guard in case the killer came back. Because Nina knew in her gut that he would return. She hoped by then she'd have backup.

She'd need it, and she'd need to pray for protection. He'd left his victim alive, and the girl had seen his face. So had Nina. She and Sam had surprised the man and thrown him off guard long enough to defuse the situation. And because of that, he'd probably come back for all of them.

* * *

US Deputy Marshal Thomas Grant brought his big Chevy pickup to a halt just off the edge of the woods. Something was certainly going on. Several police cars and a few big black SUVs sat caddy-cornered off the narrow road ahead, lights flashing to warn any passersby. Official-looking people milled around, some dressed in black and wearing FBI vests. A couple officers had K-9s with them, sniffing here and there.

He decided to investigate, because his gut told him this was more than a traffic stop or an accident. This looked like an all-out manhunt in progress.

Dressed in civilian clothes as he was, he pulled out his ID as soon as he climbed from the truck, and flashed it at the first officer he came into contact with.

"What are you doing here?" the young patrolman asked with a skeptical tone.

"Looking for a wanted man," Thomas replied on a droll note. "He could be in these parts."

The cop nodded and let him through.

Then Thomas spotted her.

A female wearing heavy jogging clothes and a bright purple wool hat hopped up out of a dark, six-foot-long hole in the snow-speckled ground. A big, fierce-looking dog met her and wagged his tail, while she held up her hands to show the crime scene techs what looked like dirt and blood.

Thomas watched as the woman talked to an officer, her hands lifted in the air. Then he glanced to where an ambulance had backed up into the woods. Two EMTs pushed a stretcher carrying a young woman hooked up to an IV toward the waiting bus.

Before he could announce his presence, the jogger glanced over at Thomas and stalked toward him. "May I ask what you're doing here, Deputy Marshal?"

He took in the light blond hair underneath the wool hat and the big brown eyes full of distrust. He had to look down at her, but she stood straight and didn't flinch.

He showed her his credentials even though he'd given the officer his name already. "US Deputy Marshal Thomas Grant. I was passing by and saw the ruckus. I'm looking for a man—."

"Hey, Nina, can you come over here?"

"Hold that thought," she told Thomas with a puzzled glare, before she turned back to a man wearing an official FBI jacket.

"Coming," she said, scooting toward where a group of FBI agents gathered by the open earth. They stood in a cluster and talked among themselves, the woman right in the middle.

Thomas waited and listened, two things he was good at. Soon enough, he'd stitched together the details. The cute blonde had been out jogging and had stumbled across a crime in progress. A man holding a gun on a young girl. The jogger must have called it in.

So the young woman was on the way to the ER and the man was long gone. And from the way the blonde was calling out information and discussing details with the K-9 agents, he'd guess she had to be someone official, too. That and the big dog shadowing her summed it up.

She was an FBI agent. And the dog was obviously her K-9 partner. Off duty and on a run, but now on full speed ahead to find the man who'd tried to kill that girl. A girl she'd obviously tried to save, from what he'd seen.

Before Thomas could corner her, someone shouted out, "Nina, we've found another body. That makes two."

"Coming, Tim." She whirled like a little cyclone and took off.

Thomas's gut burned even hotter. Two bodies and one girl shot?

Could the man who'd done this be the assassin he'd come to Montana to find?

Nina did a final sweep of the scene and then turned to leave for headquarters. She needed to file her report and meet with a sketch artist so they could get an image of the shooter to put out to the local media. The team also now had the gruesome task of helping the medical examiner to identify the two female bodies. They'd already sent out the necessary warnings and alerts to be on the look-out, and she'd talked to SAC Max West a few minutes ago to give him an update. The few agents on holiday duty had come through on doing what needed to be done, and the local sheriff's department was on it, too.

Now if she could factor in why a US Deputy Marshal had suddenly shown up, she might be able to get home and have a good night's sleep. No, that wouldn't happen. She'd seen that gunman's cold black eyes and heard that poor girl screaming. She should probably stay at headquarters and work tonight.

"Okay, Deputy Marshal Grant," she said, marching up to the tall, big-boned man wearing the suede jacket and worn jeans. "I'm Agent Nina Atkins from the FBI Tactical K-9 Unit in Billings. What's your interest in this crime scene? Did you just happen to be in the neighborhood?"

He stared her in the face with a calm scrutiny that made her shiver inside her wicking outerwear. "I happen to be here on a case. Looking for a man who could allegedly be a hired assassin, reported to possibly be last seen in Montana, near Billings. The MO mentioned here tonight sounds like his. I'd hoped you could fill me in so we can compare notes."

Suspicious, Nina gave him a long once-over while she tried to sum him up. "I'm not so sure about that."

"I know your unit," he said. "I was assigned to protecting Esme Dupree earlier this year. She was in the witness protection program, before she bolted on me. I hear she testified against her brother Reginald and that she's married to one of your team members now."

Nina gave him another scrutinizing look, surprise sparking through her system. She did hazily recall his name from that investigation, but then being a new member of the team, she hadn't been front and center on every aspect of the Dupree case, so she'd never met him. Nina felt sure she would have remembered Thomas Grant. "So, Deputy Marshal Grant—"

"Thomas," he said, his stormy gray eyes still and quiet.

"So, Thomas, tell me more about who *you're* looking for and maybe I'll share what I know." She turned to go to her SUV, thinking he'd follow her.

When she looked around to check, she found him right behind her. How did he do that without her hearing him?

"Where're we going?" he asked with a wry smile, and a husky Southern accent that shouted Texas.

"*I'm* going back to headquarters to finish out this night," she retorted. "I've got to get my partner some food and let him rest. But we can talk after I put Sam in his kennel."

She hit the fob button and the rear door to the

SUV popped open. After letting Sam inside, Nina made sure he had some water and a treat. Then she turned back to Tall, Blond and Intimidating.

She decided to stake her territory. "I need whatever information you have before I can confirm what happened here tonight."

"Of course. I'll follow you to headquarters," he said, not moving.

He looked so relaxed they could be talking about the weather. He wasn't going to give up.

"Why not tell me here?" she asked.

He glanced around and shrugged. "It's dark and cold, and if my gut is right…there's a storm coming. It's gonna be a long night. I could use some coffee and food. Y'all do have a kitchen there, right?" Then he blocked her in a going-bodyguard way. "Plus, that shooter could be watching."

Nina blinked, taking in that summary and the way his voice got all gravelly and husky again. This man made her nervous, which was silly. She didn't do nervous. But if the marshal had information on the person who'd committed this shooting, she didn't mind spending some time with him. And he had a point.

It wasn't safe in these woods.

"I've got all night," she said. "Follow me."

Thomas did as the lady asked, thinking he'd better not slip up and call her *a lady*. She'd probably deck him. If he wasn't so intent on finding Bernard Russo, he could have enjoyed getting to know Agent Nina Atkins a little better.

But that was probably a bad idea on all accounts. They both had dangerous, stressful jobs. One reason he didn't do long-term dating. That, and him being a nomad of sorts. Women wanted a settle-down kind of guy. He wasn't that.

And he had a feeling this particular woman wasn't a settle-down kind of girl, either.

Better to stick to business and get his man so he could decide where to land for the holidays. Hunting and fishing here in Montana, or maybe surfing and sailing in California? Too many options. Thomas thought about that as they traveled up the interstate to Billings.

A few minutes later, he turned into the drive leading to an impressive building in the center of the city. He'd heard the FBI Tactical K-9 Unit occupied two floors here, one for administration purposes and one for training.

Thomas followed Nina's SUV into a gated garage and found a spot two down from where she parked on the ground-floor level. They walked to the elevator together.

"The few team members we have on holiday duty are in and out," she explained. "We've had some suspicious fires in the downtown area that could be arson, but nothing much else has been going on around here until tonight."

"Well, if we're looking for the same man, your holiday duty might get a little more exciting," he replied, taking in the sight of her in the dull elevator lights.

She was buff and solid muscle, petite but with a stance that didn't mess around. Her hair shone a deep golden blond and went every which way around her face and neck. Her eyes were expressive and sparkling, a muted brown like apple cider and cinnamon.

Boy, did he have it bad. He needed to date more often. He was latching on to this woman like a puppy trying to form a bond.

Nina straightened from leaning on the elevator wall when the door opened. "I think this holiday season has already gotten exciting. We often have a lot of US Marshals coming around, but never one for Christmas. Santa must have decided I've been good this year."

Thomas had to chuckle at that sarcastic remark. Then he turned serious about what they had ahead of them. "Sorry you had to deal with this," he said. "I hope that girl makes it."

The agent gave an appreciative nod. "I'm praying for her to survive. We need to find the man who put a bullet in her shoulder."

If the man who'd shot that girl was indeed Bernard Russo, then they had a deadly killer to track down. A killer who this feisty agent had seen up close.

He could come after her.

And that would not be a good Christmas at all.

TWO

Nina sat down in a small conference room, her laptop on the table. She'd grabbed a quick shower in the locker room and put Sam in the capable hands of one of the trainers for some tender loving care. Now she was ready to get down to business. Thomas handed her a fresh cup of coffee and pulled out an electronic tablet.

"So you go first," she said, still wondering how he'd appeared out of thin air. But when she'd called Max West and given him the lowdown, the SAC had reassured her.

"Thomas Grant is a good man and one of the best in the business. He's been with the US Marshal Office for at least five years, so he's high ranking. You can take his word to the bank and, of course, he has jurisdiction in all fifty states and any US territories. Cooperate with him, but stay focused on your case. He knows to stand back and not overstep. But he is authorized to help out if he needs to. Send me the particulars, too. I can go over the reports at least. And if you need me…"

"Yes, sir. You enjoy your time with Katerina and her dad. I'll keep you posted."

Not that she minded so much that she had a US Marshal to deal with. The man was gorgeous in a way that reminded her of the movie character Thor that she and her friends drooled over. Getting her mind back to business, she let out a sigh and then stifled a yawn. "Sorry, long day. Go ahead."

Thomas opened his tablet. "Is this the man you saw tonight?"

Nina took a good look at the picture and nodded, her heart pumping as she had a flashback. "It sure looks like him. It was dark but the moon was full. He was taller than average. I remember the salt-and-pepper longish hair and the craggy skin." Then she wrapped her arms across her chest and said, "I thought you were going first."

Thomas gave her that wry smile again. "This *is* me going first. I wanted you to identify him. This is Bernard Russo. He's the man I'm looking for. We have reason to believe he's killed several people across the country from Florida to Montana, and who knows where else. He's a hired contractor. An assassin."

"And you're here to find him?"

"Yes. I got a tip that he'd possibly been sighted in Montana. Several assets reported seeing him around the state. He came here either to hide out or to take a job. He killed an informant we'd hidden to testify against a major drug ring in Texas."

"Killed, as in before you could move the informant into the witness protection program?"

"Yes, and we're not proud of it. We were moving him to a new location when someone shot out one of the tires on our transport vehicle and snatched the witness, after shooting two of our officers. They both survived, but didn't see the shooter."

"I took a different jogging path and came up on them tonight," Nina said, a delayed reaction coursing through her body. She set her coffee on the table and held her hands in her lap so he wouldn't see how they were beginning to shake. "I didn't have my weapon. Not even a Taser. I should have at least had that, or pepper spray. I didn't identify myself as FBI, but I did my best to stop him from killing her."

"You had Sam," he replied, his astute eyes watching her.

"Yes, my strongest weapon. That and lots of prayers." Sam was resting in his kennel in the training area while they talked. "I planned to order him to attack, but the man turned and shot at me and then turned the gun on the girl. Then I needed Sam to protect us while I tried to…save her."

She'd taken her shower while Thomas talked to some of the other agents, but she could still see the blood on her clothes and hands, could remember the girl's cold, pale body. A shiver moved down Nina's spine, reminding her how close that poor young woman had come to being murdered.

Help her, Lord. Help this poor girl so we can find out what's going on.

"And you *did* save her," Thomas said, as if he

knew exactly what she was thinking. "She's alive because you came along at the right time."

"She's in surgery, so let's hope everything will be okay. He planned to kill her and dump her just like the others."

"So you think the other two females were killed by this same man?"

"I don't know. I'm speculating. But it makes sense because he purposely brought her to that spot, from what we can tell. I'm waiting to hear from the medical examiner regarding their cause of death and their IDs. We'll have to notify their next of kin, too."

"A grisly undertaking," Thomas replied. "My gut tells me Russo is your man for all three crimes."

"I'll have to wait to concur with you on that, but yes, it's looking like a possibility."

He nodded. "Understood."

She leaned forward. "Sam must have picked up a strong scent, because after the shooter shot the girl and ran away, Sam immediately alerted on the two other graves. Shallow graves, a little over a foot and a half deep. The gunman knew that would keep anyone from detecting the scent of decaying bodies. Until Sam got a whiff anyway. I can't say how long they've been there, but the ME said maybe months."

Putting her head in her hands and raking her wet hair back, she said, "Sam and I have jogged by those woods for months now and...those girls were out there. All alone. Now, I'm questioning if Sam tried to alert me before and I maybe thought he'd seen a squirrel or some other animal. I should have caught this sooner." Lifting her head, she added, "The killer must be using that site as his burial ground since, according to the ME, one body has been there longer than the other one."

"Sam knows his business. He wasn't working when you jogged by before and he could have false alerted, since he was on downtime. But tonight, like you said, he picked up on the dangerous situation. The shooter's scent—maybe a cologne or aftershave, or maybe even from the coat he was wearing—caused Sam to search the area, and then he alerted on the bodies. Which makes it highly likely the same man killed those two."

"Not good news for any family, especially this time of year."

"No," the marshal said, his expression grim. "But it sounds as if you have a strong faith to carry you through. That's a plus."

"I couldn't do this without it," she admitted.

"I hear that," he said, that long Texas drawl moving like gentle fingers across her heart.

Nina didn't talk about her faith much but it was there, instilled in her by a strong, loving family. She was glad to hear Thomas apparently had the same shield.

They continued to talk about the details until

she'd given him as much information as she could and he'd done the same for her.

"I think I'm going home," she said, standing to stretch. "I'll pick back up on the details there, since I probably won't get any sleep."

"I've got a room at the Wild Iris Inn," he said. "Sounded like a nice out-of-the-way spot. I didn't want to stay in Billings."

"The inn is the only place available near Iris Rock, and not far from my house," she said with a grin. "But you're in good hands. Miss Claire still works there part-time, but she's turned over management to Penny Potter, soon to be Penny Morrow. Penny plans to marry one of our agents—Zeke Morrow—on Valentine's Day next year."

She went on to tell him how Jake Morrow had been a double agent and how his half brother, Zeke, had come to help track him and had been in on his capture and death. But in spite of the horrible tragedy, several of the team members had somehow found true love. Why Nina had decided to share the joy with the marshal, she didn't know. Except that she wanted to believe in hope and love, even if she didn't have a significant other in her life right now.

And she didn't need anyone. She had enough trouble trying to prove herself as an agent.

"This year was rough for all of you," Thomas said, bringing her back to reality. "I'm glad everyone is safe and sound." They'd reached the doors to the parking garage. "Speaking of that, I'm walking you to your vehicle."

Nina blinked and stared up at him. "I'm parked near you, anyway, and I have Sam."

Thomas shook his head. "Look, let's get this part over with. I know you're strong and capable and tough or you wouldn't be here, but…a killer saw you tonight. You're a witness to an attempted murder by a very dangerous man. You're gonna need someone to watch your back."

She turned when they were almost to her vehicle. "Have you appointed yourself for that job?"

Before he could respond, a shot rang out and the windshield of the car next to them shattered. Thomas threw his body over Nina and pushed her to the ground. Another shot rang out, blasting a nearby wall.

Nina's heart pressed beats against her lungs. She couldn't breathe. And she couldn't get past the sure knowledge that Thomas had probably just saved her life.

An hour later, Nina and Thomas were back inside headquarters filing yet another report, and Thomas was now a partner in this investigation. He didn't mind that, since he needed to be a part of it if Russo was involved.

But that hadn't been established. This pattern didn't match Russo's way of taking care of business.

The shooter was nowhere to be found, and surveillance cameras didn't show anyone sneaking into the garage. So the shooter must have had a good view of where they were parked from an off-site spot. They'd canvassed the whole place and the surrounding buildings, and they'd put out more alerts on Russo. The techs were still trying to establish where he'd been hidden. But the destruction from the shots indicated a shotgun. Which meant he'd been close. Too close.

"He's after you," Thomas said to Nina, when they were alone. "You can't go back to your place tonight."

"I'll bunk here," Nina retorted, obviously not in the mood to be told what to do. "I've done it before. And I intend to keep digging. Dylan O'Leary is our best tech and he'll be back on this tomorrow. He'll do research based on what you've told us. Thanks for your help."

Thomas put his hands on his hips. "Are you dismissing me, Agent Atkins?"

She gave him a tired glare. "It's almost two in the morning. Don't you ever sleep?"

"Do you?"

She stood and paced, her green sweater long and droopy, her jeans old and worn. Locker clothes. But she looked cute in them. "Have you considered that he might have been aiming at you, Thomas?"

He rubbed his jaw. "Always a possibility, and

yes, he could have taken both of us out and called it a day. But he missed, which is kind of surprising."

"Do you think he blinked, got the shakes?"

Thomas figured this man knew how to use any kind of weapon. "He could have been interrupted or startled, but why a shotgun? Maybe the darkness and seeing both of us together shook him. He sure wasn't expecting to see me here."

"Now he knows you're in town," she said, her fingers twisting in the cuffs of her sweater. "You might need to bunk here tonight, too."

Thomas hadn't planned on that. "I could hang around."

"That's not what I said."

"And I'm saying I can hang around." Seeing the objection on her heart-shaped face, he held up his hands in defense. "Hey, neither of us is gonna get much sleep. We can get a head start on the facts and get our ducks in a row."

She stared at him, her eyes changing so swiftly he felt as if he was chasing glints of pure copper. "Are you hungry?" she finally asked.

Did this mean she would listen to reason and let him do his job?

"Starving. That snack cake I found in the machine went stale in my stomach a couple hours ago."

"I think we have leftover hamburgers in the fridge. Somebody brought in a whole dozen or so from our favorite downtown eatery."

"Sounds good. Lead me to the kitchen."

Nina shot him another mixed-message glance. "We're in this together now, Deputy Marshal. And I have orders from my SAC to cooperate with you whether I like it or not."

"Won't be the first time a woman has tried to resist my charms," he quipped, hoping to lighten the mood.

"I'm an agent first," she retorted. "And a woman second."

Okey-dokey. "Whatever you say, ma'am."

Thomas followed her through the maze of offices and cubicles, thinking at least he had someone interesting to work with. This one would try her best to keep him on his toes.

And he'd try his best to keep her alive.

THREE

"The girl's awake."

Nina rose from her chair, boots hitting the floor, and followed Dylan O'Leary, the agency's tech expert, down the hallway. "Is she talking?"

Thomas saw them and came out of the chair he'd found in a corner of the big cubicle-filled room. "Identity?"

Dylan kept right on going, his glasses stuck to his nose as always. "Kelly Denton. Twenty-four years old. College student who grew up in Helena and worked for former State Senator Richard Slaton. She'd moved away from Helena this year but went home to visit her parents for Christmas. They've verified that and said she had left a message that she was spending the night with a friend. That was night before last. They're on their way here." Dylan hurried off and then turned back around. "Oh, and don't mention the other girls to her yet. We're still trying to establish if they're connected. She could voluntarily fill in the blanks."

"Got it. We're on our way to investigate." Nina turned to Thomas. "Ready to question our witness?"

"Been ready," he said, grabbing his coat.

Soon, they were in Nina's SUV headed east to the Billings Medical Center.

"How'd you sleep?" Nina asked, recalling how she'd tossed and turned and had nightmares the entire three hours she'd tried to sleep.

"Like a baby," he quipped with a wry smile. "I was exhausted after that long drive from Texas."

"Why'd you drive across the country in the dead of winter?"

"I like long drives. Helps me think. Plus I was trying to track Russo's every step so I could establish that he drove here, too. Found some rental cars he'd used here and there, but nothing concrete. So you didn't see or hear him leaving in a vehicle last night?"

Nina shook her head and merged into traffic. "Nope. He ran away, headed into the woods. I still don't get it. He could have shot me, too."

"Maybe Sam distracted him. Sam would have gone after him, don't you think?"

"Possibly. I'm sure he'd have brought down the man. But I was worried that he'd shoot Sam and return to finish the job. Why do you think he ran like that?"

"He panicked. He wasn't expecting anyone to stumble on the scene."

"Yes. Sam and I did surprise him. I know the woods beyond that spot and across the stream are on private property. Someone owns a hunting lodge up there. He could have hidden in it, possibly, but until we find out who owns that place, we can't get a warrant to look."

"But he shot at you—shot at us—last night," Thomas reminded her. "And missed. Russo's trained never to miss. Something's not right about this whole thing."

"I'm kind of glad he missed," Nina replied, wondering what was bugging Thomas. "So...we both think something's off here, right?"

"He's after Kelly. We'll have to watch the hospital. He might be trying to distract us while he moves in on her."

"We *do* have her surrounded," Nina said. "Agents twenty-four/seven, guarding her room."

"I hope that will keep Russo away."

Thomas didn't sound so confident, but they were dealing with a trained assassin. Nina couldn't blame the marshal for being concerned. "Remember, for all he knows she's dead. We only broadcasted that we were looking for him. Not that he'd tried to kill someone."

"But that kind of news tends to leak," Thomas replied. "We might need to move her, and quickly."

They made it to the hospital without incident and were inside safe and sound in under an hour.

After getting permission from the hospital staff to interrogate Kelly Denton, they went into her room. The guard at the door was a massive sheriff deputy. No one would get past that man.

Nina approached the pale young girl, remembering her there in the moonlight last night. The bullet had just missed her heart and had become lodged in her left shoulder, but the surgery had gone as well as could be expected. Her prognosis was good, barring the killer didn't come back. Now if they could match that bullet the surgeon had dug out to the gun that shot her, they'd have an idea what kind of weapon the killer was carrying. A stretch, but something to hope for.

"Kelly, do you remember me?" Nina asked, hoping the girl would recognize her.

She moved her head and stared with bleary eyes. "I… I don't know."

"I saw you last night with that man…"

The girl's face turned deadly pale and all the numbers and graphs on the monitor jittered and changed. "He tried to kill me."

"I know," Nina said, glancing to where Thomas stood by the closed drapery over the window. "I was jogging and I came upon you."

"You saved my life."

"I tried to stop him," Nina said. "But he shot at me and he *did* shoot you." Touching Kelly's hand, she said, "Can you tell us how you wound up with him, so far from Helena?"

"He…he took me when I was walking to my car," the girl said, her whispers full of fear. "I'd just left a restaurant. He was waiting with an open van and he had a gun."

Nina wrote down the name of the place. "And he drove you here to Billings?"

"Yes, he tied me up and put a blindfold on me. I was in the back—a small van."

"Do you know the color or model?"

"No. He shoved me inside and put the blindfold on me and then tied me up. I couldn't get to my purse or phone." She tried to sit up, her eyes wild now. "Where is my phone? I need my phone."

"We didn't find your purse or phone," Nina said, gently lowering her back down. "He probably tossed them."

Thomas shot Nina a knowing glance. "Can you tell us anything else, Kelly?"

The girl lay still, her fingers clutching the light blanket spread over her. Nina glanced at Thomas. She'd worked with enough traumatized women to know when someone was truly terrified.

"He kept asking about a key," Kelly said in a weak voice, her gaze darting down and to the left. "I don't know what he was talking about. I don't know anything. I shouldn't have gone back there."

"Back where?" Thomas asked.

"To Helena. I—I should have stayed away. When can I go home?"

Thomas stepped away from the window. The girl's vitals were going crazy. "Are you sure you don't remember something? A detail we could use?" he asked, keeping his gaze on the beeping machines. "Were you in danger before you left Helena?"

Kelly gripped the blankets, clutching them like

a lifeline. "No. I can't talk about this. I just want to go home. When are my parents coming?"

A nurse came in, her expression stern. "Time's up."

"Your parents are on their way," Nina said, wishing she could comfort the girl more and find out what she seemed so afraid of. "You're safe here. We have a guard on your room."

"Is he coming back?" Kelly asked, fear in her eyes. "That man? If he does, he'll kill me! He told me he'd kill me."

"Not if we can help it," Thomas said, honesty in each word. "If you remember anything—or decide to tell us the truth—please tell the deputy and he'll alert us. The more we know, the sooner we can end this and then you'll be safe."

The girl didn't seem so sure. She was frightened, and for good reason. Nina talked to the deputy and felt reassured when he told her one of her team members would be here later with his K-9 partner.

Nina tugged at Thomas's jacket sleeve when they reached the elevator. "Let's stay here a while. We can see her door from the waiting room. And…we can talk to her parents after they arrive and they've seen her. Maybe they can shed some light on whatever she's not telling us."

He nodded. "Okay, but I'm hungry. Let's go down to the cafeteria."

"Didn't you eat one of those pastries from Petrov Bakery? Or maybe even two?"

He gave her a mock frown. "That was breakfast."

"Yes, only two hours ago."

"I have to be fed every two hours."

Nina snorted and shook her head. "Right." Then she said, "Okay, we'll get you fed, but then I'm hanging out here. I'm worried about that girl."

"She's hiding something, no doubt," Thomas said, turning serious in that lightning quick way she'd noticed. "She said she should never have gone back to Helena. She knows about the key and she panicked when she realized she didn't have her phone."

"And you can read minds?" Nina asked in surprise. But she had to agree with him.

"I can read people," Thomas replied. "That girl is scared, of course. But it's more. I think she purposely dropped that bit about the key to give us a hint. She's terrified and that's understandable, but she said she didn't know *anything*. Which to me means she knows a lot."

"You have a point," Nina said, as they hurried through the buffet line. She got a salad and Thomas ordered meat loaf, mashed potatoes with gravy and a giant biscuit. The man knew how to down some serious food. How did he stay in such good shape? "She did seem pretty emphatic about not knowing anything."

"My gut is burning," he retorted.

"Maybe that's just the pastries and the meat loaf," she said with a grin.

"Ha, ha." He chewed on a chunk of meat loaf before he answered. "No, this is my gut telling me I'm right."

"Are you always right?"

"Not always. But about 99 percent of the time."

She had to laugh. He made her do that. "Tell me about you, Deputy Marshal. So I get from the accent and the way you can go all cowboy that you grew up in Texas."

He leaned close, his gray eyes twinkling. "Why, yes ma'am, I sure did. Texas through and through. Went to college in Austin, got my degree in criminal justice, worked in law enforcement in several capacities, applied to become a US Marshal and I've been one for five years now. Based out of Florida for a while, but I had a hankering to come back West."

His smile was pro but his eyes went beyond professional. They turned all smoky and flirtatious in a quicksilver way that made her insides shake like the Jell-O the man at the next table was trying to eat.

"You like your job, don't you?" she asked, to keep the conversation moving. To make his eyes change back to a safe level of gray.

"I do. I mean, chasing bad guys, yeah, what's not to like?"

Nodding, she laughed at that. "Same here. I love being a K-9 officer for the FBI."

"It's dangerous work."

"You mean for a woman."

"I mean for anyone."

Then he did the stern, serious thing again. "What put that chip on your shoulder?"

"Oh, you mean the chip about how hard it is to be a woman in what most consider a man's profession?"

"Yeah, that one."

"I told you I come from a big family, right?"

"Yes."

"Well, I have four brothers. All in law enforcement."

"Ouch. So you joined up because you had to prove yourself to them."

"And to my father, who is a retired sheriff."

"Whoa. Can't they see how good you are at your job?"

"No, what they see is their little sister trying to do a job they think is not suitable for her. And... they're all kind of jealous that I'm in this elite FBI unit when they're locals who work hard."

"They should be proud of you," Thomas said, the passion in his words shaking her. "I never had much of a family. My parents divorced when I was little and I kind of got shoved from my grandparents to my aunts and uncles. My dad worked construction and traveled a little too much, and my mom skipped out on me once they got divorced."

Nina's heart did a little flip. No wonder the man moved around like a nomad. "Do you ever go back to Texas?"

"Yeah. My granddad left me a small ranch there. I head straight to it when I need some downtime. He was a good man, a churchgoer, just not an affectionate man."

Nina wanted to keep talking, but they needed to get back. She stood up and said, "Well, remember, if we get through this, you are definitely coming to my family's house for Christmas."

Then she realized she'd overstepped and wished she could take it back. Maybe they'd be done before Christmas.

He grinned, which only made him even more handsome. "Oh, so you want to make those ornery brothers even more jealous. I mean, who wouldn't be impressed with a US Marshal, right?"

She shook her head at his antics. "Right."

They'd just turned the corner back to the waiting area when a male nurse hurried up to the guard at Kelly Denton's door. When the nurse saw them, he took off running in the other direction.

FOUR

Thomas went into action, tackling the man dressed in hospital scrubs in time to stop him from getting away. Another nurse immediately called security. The hospital would go on lockdown until they cleared this up.

The deputy who'd been guarding Kelly's room didn't miss a beat. He helped Thomas by putting a heavy, booted foot on the man's backbone while Thomas grabbed his hands and cuffed him. Together, they lifted him up and slammed him down in a nearby chair. Thomas searched his scrubs and found a small knife.

Nina held her gun on the man until she knew he was secure. "I'll check on the girl."

By now, nurses and doctors were merging inside the room where Kelly Denton lay sleeping. She woke with a start, her eyes wide. "What's going on?"

"Everything's okay," Nina said, thinking they should have stayed close by. But at least they had a suspect now. Only the man they'd tackled wasn't Russo. "Just a ruckus outside. You're safe." Better not to upset her again so soon.

But she had to wonder if the girl needed to be moved again.

When the medical team had checked and rechecked Kelly, her parents came in. After they'd seen her and were reassured she was on the mend, Nina took them outside and explained what had happened.

"Do you know of any reason someone would want to harm your daughter?" she asked.

"No," they both replied.

"But she's been away for almost a year," her mom added. "Maybe someone followed her to Helena?"

"It's your job to find that out," Mr. Denton said. "I thought she was being protected."

"She is. We've taken the man into custody, but he's not talking. He won't tell us who hired him, but he's not going anywhere, I promise."

"They could send someone else," Kelly's mother whispered, tears in her eyes. "Can't we take her home to Helena?"

Nina glanced at Thomas, who had joined them. He frowned and pondered that. "The doctors aren't ready to release her yet, but when they do, we'll have to send someone with her if the man who shot her is still at large. Do you have any other place you could take her for a few days?"

"My parents live about thirty miles from Helena in a gated community. We could take her there," Mrs. Denton offered.

"I'll call ahead when it's time and if it comes to that," Thomas said. "She could become a possible witness in a federal case. We can help protect her here and…we might have to put her into witness protection if this drags out too long."

The Dentons both seemed confused and frightened by that. "You don't mean forever, do you?" her mother asked with tears in her eyes.

Nina shot Thomas a thankful glance. "We hope it won't come to that. For now, we'll be in touch to coordinate things as soon as she's clear to leave the hospital. And we'll have someone here to escort all of you to your destination."

"Meantime, we have the deputy and a K-9 team member here, so she'll have two people guarding her door at all times," Thomas added. "And if she tells either of you anything, please let us know. We can't help her if we don't know what we're dealing with."

Kelly's parents nodded, but they looked shell-shocked.

"We can also have her moved to another room," Nina said, promising to talk to the hospital administrators.

She and Thomas went to take care of the details. Soon, everything was in place to move Kelly to a room near the nurses' station, where she could be monitored more closely by both the guards and the staff.

Having assured her parents that Kelly would be safe, and telling them they'd be watched, too, Nina and the marshal went back to headquarters, hoping to question the man they'd taken into custody.

Three hours later, after questioning the non-communicative suspect and then going over files and trying to establish leads, all they had to go on was the suspect's rap sheet of petty crime, and the fact that he refused to give them any information. Robby Collier was a local who'd been minding his own business in a bar when he'd been offered a job paying a huge amount of money.

He regretted that decision, but said he couldn't tell them anything more. "The man made it pretty clear if I got caught, I was on my own. I don't know nothing except I was supposed to take down the guard at the door."

"I guess you didn't think that part through, either," Nina had noted, before they left him locked up tight.

"He thinks he's safer in lockup than out there," Thomas said now. "This has Russo all over it. He hired someone to bring down the guard, which means he was probably in the hospital, too. I'm surprised he didn't shoot dear Robby on the spot for failing in his mission."

"But they locked the place down," Nina said, regretting that she'd left Sam with the handlers here while they'd gone to the hospital. Sam could have helped chase down the assailant. "He had to get away quick. Why would he send someone so unreliable and, well, green?"

"He messed up and left a witness, something he's never done before. And now, because of one determined K-9 officer, he wants this over and done. He has to know you're FBI by now. You're both still in danger."

"So because the heat's on, he turned to desperate measures and sent that clown to do his dirty work," Nina said.

"Russo knows how to get away in a hurry," Thomas pointed out. "He wouldn't hang around since this mission got botched, too. But…he's not going to give up. Like our Robby, he knows he's in serious danger himself. Whoever hired him has been informed by now that things went bad."

"But how did he know the girl wasn't dead? We haven't released any details to the press."

"The crime scene," Thomas said. "It was active and it got a lot of attention. Anyone could have seen the first responders carting Kelly away. I walked right up. A reporter or newshound could have easily done the same."

"Russo could have still been hanging around, too," she said, glad Sam had picked up his scent. But then, Sam did specialize in cadaver detection and he'd done that job to perfection last night. After that, a lot of people had passed through those woods.

Tired and unable to gather her thoughts, Nina stood up and stretched. "I'm going home tonight. Tim and Zeke checked my place and it's safe. No one's been there that we can tell."

"That you know of," Thomas retorted. "You're safer here."

"I'm safe at my house, too," she replied. "I have security and I have Sam. And I have several weapons."

"A woman after my own heart," he deadpanned. "I'll be two miles down the road, letting Penny Potter and the Wild Iris staff pamper me."

"Good." She kind of wished he'd offered to at least come to her house for coffee. But then, they'd both drunk enough of that dark brew... and she had to resist whatever was brewing between them, too. "I'm going to decorate the tree I brought home the other day before all the needles fall off, and make myself a big cup of hot chocolate. Maybe watch a sappy Christmas movie just for kicks."

In reality she'd grab some popcorn and go back over this bizarre case. But he didn't need to know that.

They walked out together, both searching the area for another sniper, Sam trotting at their feet and two armed guards set up in the parking garage. When they reached their vehicles, Thomas turned to her. "I'm kind of lonely, you know. I haven't had a real Christmas in years. I'd enjoy helping you decorate that dying tree."

Nina's heart betrayed her by bouncing all around her chest. "Are you inviting yourself to dinner, Thomas?"

"Are you asking me to dinner, Nina?"

"No."

He laughed. "Then yes, I'm inviting myself to dinner, but I really only wanted to decorate the tree. But if you insist…"

"I don't recall insisting."

"But you were thinking it, right?"

She wondered how he did that. No wonder bad guys tried to steer clear of him.

"No," she said with a laugh, "I was thinking too bad I don't cook."

He leaned close, his whisper half a step away. "Even better. I do."

She'd never had a man cook for her before. Should she tell him to get lost? Or should she let him follow her home so they could brainstorm this case all over again?

She glanced down at the rottweiler. "What do you think, Sam? Should Thomas cook us dinner, but only because we want to pick his brain later and try to figure out things on this investigation?"

The big dog looked from her to the marshal and let out a woof.

"I think that was a yes," Thomas said, his handsome face full of a triumphant smugness.

"Only because it's Christmas and you're a stranger in a strange land."

"I hear that," he replied. Then he scanned the parking garage. "We sure don't need to be standing here out in the open arguing about it, so let's go."

* * *

Nina turned off the security alarm and rushed inside the tiny cottage she'd lived in since she'd arrived in Iris Rock a few months ago. The drive to and from Billings could be tricky on a night such as this, when a new snowfall seemed imminent. But she'd grown up in the bitter cold of Wyoming and knew how to mount snow tires on her vehicle and how to use her head and her driving skills while braking. She was pretty capable at most things, except when it came to kitchen duty. But she wasn't really serious about letting Thomas cook for her.

"What was I thinking?" she asked Sam. He shadowed her, hoping for his own dinner. "I don't have food and I don't cook. I can't offer him your dinner, right?"

The dog shot her a doleful glance that stated *"Nope."*

Knowing Thomas would be close behind her, she tidied up, clearing away the local paper and some research books and novels off the couch, then hurried to change into jeans and a blue-and-white-striped wool sweater. She was running a comb through her tousled hair and putting on pink lip gloss when the doorbell rang.

She'd never actually invited anyone here before. Especially not a man.

"Mom would be proud," she whispered to Sam.

Sam woofed a positive approval that the person at her door came in peace.

But she checked the peephole, anyway.

Too much tall stood there.

Now she was sweating in her sweater.

"C'mon in," she said, her words deceitfully calm. "I'm going to be honest. I'm not sure I have anything on hand to make an edible meal."

Shrugging out of his heavy coat, Thomas took in the small living room and galley kitchen. Nina watched him for signs of disappointment or regret. But in typical lawman fashion, he seemed to be sizing up security—and taking in information on how she lived.

Heavy beige curtains covered the sliding doors to the tiny backyard that she and Sam loved to play in. The furniture came with the place, and it was mismatched and clunky.

Wishing she'd taken a little time to decorate the rooms with her own sense of style, Nina crossed her arms over her midsection and stood her ground. She worked too much to worry about making it into *Architectural Digest*.

"It ain't much, but it's home," she chirped, motioning to the big doors and several windows. "On good days, I can see the Pryor Mountains, which is kind of cool since I could also see them from my bedroom in Wyoming, growing up."

His stormy eyes widened. "What, you circled the mountain and settled on the other side?"

"Something like that." Looking at her sad little home through the eyes of someone else made Nina self-conscious and almost embarrassed. But she shook that off the way she shook off everything she couldn't deal with. "Let's see what we can round up."

She headed to the refrigerator and stared at the barren shelves. "I see a few carrots and two potatoes." Then she checked the freezer. "And a bag of chicken breasts that might have come with the house."

Thomas snorted and gently moved her aside. "The date on the chicken is still within the safe zone. We'll hope the same with the potatoes and carrots. Do you stock any canned goods?"

She nodded and opened an overhead cabinet by the refrigerator. "Oh, look, chicken noodle soup and tomato soup. If only we had some crackers."

"We don't need crackers," he stated, already rolling up his sleeves. "You get the decorations ready and I'll get dinner going."

"What exactly do you plan to cook?" she asked, wondering how she'd managed to get in this predicament in the first place.

"The Thomas Grant special, ma'am," he said in his best Texas drawl. "You're gonna love it."

She doubted that, but she'd give it a shot since she couldn't kick him out now. Sam's head moved in ping-pong style back and forth between them.

Obviously, he smelled something in the air. Something distinctive and different.

Another human in the kitchen. Or a tad too much of some new and exciting undercurrent.

Soon, Thomas had the chicken and potatoes browning in a big pot, along with some onions and peppers he'd discovered in a crisper drawer with all the joy of a kid opening a present. He hummed while he cooked.

Nina pretended to be unraveling Christmas lights, but she couldn't help glancing over at him. A giant wearing boots had taken over her home. And it was beginning to smell good, which caused her stomach to make strange noises and her heart to do funny jumps and bumps.

Finally, after he'd dismantled cans and rummaged for spices and splashed this and that into the pot, he turned it to simmer and came to sit beside her on the now-too-small floral love seat in front of the tiny electric fireplace. "Chicken noodle soup and biscuits coming up in about a half hour."

"Really?" she asked, surprised. "We could have just opened a can for the soup. And I'm not sure how you managed biscuits."

"Really, I opened two cans for my special soup. And added a few special ingredients."

"I'm almost afraid to ask."

"Then don't."

"And the biscuits?"

"You had flour, milk, eggs and baking powder."

"My mom restocks every time she comes to visit."

"Well, that turned out to be a good thing."

His eyes were so amazing. They'd turned as blue-gray as the storm she'd seen over the big sky at dusk and just as mysterious.

Nina laughed and inhaled. "Well, I have to admit that smells better than the soggy pizza I usually bring home."

"You're almost out of protein bars," he replied. "I didn't throw your last two into the pot."

"I'm so glad you didn't."

They bantered back and forth while they got the lights straightened out and wrapped around the sad little evergreen.

"I think this tree is going to be lost in a burst of color," Thomas stated. "Where did you buy it? 'Cause I think you need a refund."

"Ha, funny." She shrugged. "A kid was selling them to make money to buy a bicycle. I felt sorry for him. He'd obviously scoured the back forty and…found the best of the lot."

"We could find you a prettier tree," Thomas pointed out. "But this one is kind of tugging at my heartstrings in that Charlie Brown kind of way."

"I wish you could see the tree my mom and dad put up each year," she replied, not even thinking about her words. "It's fresh and has to be at least nine feet tall and covers one corner of the den in our log house. Dad fusses every year, but he loves hanging the lights on the tree and along the staircase. We all gather on Christmas Eve and sing carols and hymns, and then we eat a big meal of barbecue and all the trimmings. My brothers and their families all live nearby and I usually show up at the last minute and then…it's Christmas."

"That *is* Christmas," Thomas said, his eyes dark with a longing that tore at Nina's heart. "Sounds wonderful."

"You'll see, Thomas," she said. "My family has a steadfast rule that we can bring anyone we want home for Christmas."

He nodded, but he didn't look so sure about that invitation.

Did he think she was pushing him in the wrong way? Nina wondered. Because she'd done it again. Invited him to go home with her for Christmas. She wouldn't ask anymore.

Or was he too afraid to stop being alone to enjoy being with someone during the holidays?

She was about to ask him that when the buzzer on the stove dinged and caused her to step back.

"Dinner is ready," he said, that distant longing still in his eyes, his smile beautiful but full of resolve and regret. "We'd better eat so we can finish making this tree as special as the one you just described."

FIVE

"I have to admit, that was some pretty good soup. Noodles and potatoes and carrots and…what kind of spices did you put in there?"

Thomas grinned and winked. "You had some ginger and rosemary stashed away in the spice drawer."

Nina hit a hand against her head. "Oh, my mom gave me a whole spice rack last time I was home. I think she was trying to give me a hint. You know, get some spice in your life and find someone and get married and make babies."

"All that from a couple of shakes into the pot?"

"All that and more," she replied, before taking a sip of her hot chocolate. "She also gave me this cocoa mix."

He toasted her with his own. "I think mixing up the recipe in a Mason jar is sweet. It's a mama thing."

Remembering he'd never had that, she nodded. "I have a good family so I shouldn't complain."

Misreading her statement for pity, he put down the mug with a motif of a laughing reindeer centered on it. "Hey, don't apologize or downplay that on my account. I'm okay. I have a good job and I get to travel the whole country having fun."

"Fun? You call some of the things we deal with fun?"

"No. I said I was having fun, not that it is fun."

"Oh, so that makes a big difference."

"I love my job," he admitted with a sheepish shrug. "If I can't have a big family, I can help someone else get home to theirs."

"I guess that's a good way to look at it," she replied, turning serious while her heart did that strange little beat again. "Except those two dead girls never had that chance."

"We'll find him," Thomas said. "I have a steadfast rule. I always get the bad guy."

"I try to enforce that same rule," she said. "But I'm still new to the team. I've been here almost a year now and things are getting better, but I never wanted to up my status by stumbling into something this twisted and strange."

"You were the first officer on the scene. Your SAC is wise to stand back and let you do your job."

"Maybe," she said. And then she asked Thomas something she'd been wondering. "But is he doing that because of my abilities or because *you* just happened along to help out?"

Surprise filled Thomas's eyes. "Does it matter? We're in it together now."

She stood and took their empty mugs to the

sink. "But would I be carrying the same clout if you weren't here?"

Irritation shadowed his expression. "Are we seriously having this conversation? Am I a threat to you, Nina?"

"No. But am I an equal to you?"

"You're way above my pay scale, even if you earn less than me," he said, gathering his coat. "I came here for one reason—to bring a killer back to Texas. I can't change the circumstances that brought us together, but I intend to do my job. But you seem to have a one track mind on getting bad guys, so that makes you more valuable than me right now."

In spite of you, she figured he wanted to say. He intended to do his job in spite of her.

Wishing she'd kept her mouth shut, Nina pushed at her hair and then tugged at her sweater. "I'm sorry. I want to do my job, too."

"Then cut that kind of talk," he said, jamming his meaty arms into his coat. "It's been a long day. I think I'll head back to the inn. I would offer to check the place, but I don't want to offend your stubborn need to measure up."

She deserved that, Nina decided. Why had she even let him see her insecurities? That only made her look weak and helpless.

"Thanks, Thomas," she said in a low voice. "For helping with the tree and…for cooking."

"You can enjoy the leftovers tomorrow night," he retorted.

Alone.

The silence shouted that one word between them.

He turned for the door, Nina close behind.

And then the whole house went black.

Sam growled quietly. Nina didn't move, but she crouched low next to her partner. Listening, she heard a noise out in the carport attached to the house. It sounded as if someone had stumbled into the empty trash can. Then she heard the groan of something heavy being shoved aside.

The rottweiler woofed. "Sam, quiet," she ordered. "Stay."

She could hear Thomas by the door. "Nina, stay down."

"I am down," she whispered. "But I don't have my weapon and I never reset the alarm after we came in tonight."

"I've got my weapon," he said. "And he'd have probably disengaged the alarm, anyway."

He came near and grasped her by the arm. "It could be the storm. Where's your circuit breaker?"

"The kitchen, by the door to the carport. But I heard something—"

"I did, too."

"Let's check."

He didn't argue. Together, they stayed down

and worked their way to the kitchen. Nina sat and scooted toward the corner where the circuit box was located. "I'll need some light," she whispered.

Thomas followed her and pulled out his phone and handed it to her. Using the faint moonlight creeping through the shuttered blinds, she found the flashlight app and slowly worked her way up the wall.

But before she could check the circuit breaker, the door right beside her jiggled and a shot rang out, splintering the wood and sending fragments flying as Thomas threw her to the floor.

"He's bold," the marshal said, sitting up with his weapon drawn.

"Shoot," she suggested, wishing she had her own gun.

Thomas got in front of Nina on one knee and shot back, adding more bullet holes to the shattered wood.

"I guess if he's dead, we'll have to explain," she whispered. "But I would technically be protecting my castle."

"I'll go and find him," Thomas suggested instead. "If I didn't get him already."

Nina thought about what she'd have done if Thomas hadn't been here. She would have grabbed her weapon and taken control. "Or I could open the door and let Sam do his job."

"Good idea. But both those strategies are risky."

"We need to call for backup."

"The best plan. And if they don't make it in time, I'm shooting to kill."

That's what she would have done. Weapon, backup, shoot to defend and protect.

She made the call with his phone, giving her name, rank and location.

When they heard a bang against the glass sliding doors, Nina ordered Sam to bark and guard. The dog headed in that direction, sounding every bit as fierce as he looked.

"Guess I missed," Thomas said.

"He won't give up," Nina replied.

"What is he doing here?" the marshal retorted. "He has to know we're both in here and armed."

"And that I have security. Not that it matters now."

"He's prowling, for some reason. He didn't get to Kelly, so now he's after us."

Another shot streaked through the air, this time shattering a window just above their heads.

Nina jumped up and looked through the slats of the blinds. "If I can see him, I might be able to ID him as the man in the woods."

"He's toying with us," Thomas answered. "To flush us out."

"He'll shoot us both if we try to get out. And if we don't, he'll keep shooting until he hits one of us."

"Agreed…" The big man shifted and eyed the side door that held a scatter-shot scar. "I'm not sure what his plan is, but he's angry, so he's enjoying this."

Nina moved around the small area where they were crouched. She stood, but Thomas pulled her back down. "Don't try to locate him. He'll be expecting that."

"I wasn't," she said in a weak whisper. "I wanted to grab the hot chocolate my mom made. I don't want it to get shot."

Thomas fell for her just a little bit more after that soft-spoken confession. But he had to protect the stubborn woman so they could share that hot chocolate.

"We'll worry about that later," he said, holding her down. "We'll have to sit right here until help comes."

"I don't want to sit," she replied. "Let me go around the house and at least try to find him. Sam will show me the trail." Sam stood guarding the sliding glass doors.

"We wait until we can't take it anymore," he replied. "It's too risky."

"But I need my weapon. It's what I'd do if I were here alone. I'd get to my weapon and go after him."

"But you're not alone, and right now, I don't want to argue about it."

Nina squirmed and held on to the jar of hot

chocolate. "I don't like your being here, but I'm glad you are."

"You are a paradox," he retorted.

Sam's woofs sounded like questions. *"What's the plan?"*

"I vote we make a run for it now," Nina said, her tone decisive. "I won't sit here and wait to die."

"Okay." Thomas helped her up and gave her his coat. "Put this on. We'll go out the kitchen door and use our vehicles as a shield if he starts shooting."

"That'll work," she said, already preparing. She summoned Sam and ordered him to guard. "For now," she told Thomas.

The marshal went ahead and slowly cracked open the side door. The burst of cold air nearly took his breath away, but the blast of the next shot caused him to duck down and slam the door again.

"Are you sure you want to go out there?" he asked Nina.

"What choice do we have?"

"Once we get out, I can circle back and take him," Thomas replied. "If he's still here."

Nina nodded, concern in her eyes. At least she hadn't argued with him.

While Nina hadn't parked her vehicle under the carport, she had pulled it up alongside the open garage. But when Thomas tried to open the door again, and wider this time, it moved only a couple inches.

"He's blocked us in. What do you have in that trash can?"

"I just emptied it," she said. Then she let out a breath. "I have a potting bench right next to it. He must have wedged it against the can."

"Nina?"

She eyed the situation from behind him and then carefully placed her hot chocolate mix in a nearby cabinet. "We're trapped," she said, her tone calm, all things considered. "He's trapping us until he can find a way in."

"But *we'll* find a way *out*," Thomas said. "If I can shove the table away a few more inches and we run fast, we might be able to get out before he returns to the garage. He must be making his way around the house and back."

"It's that or die trying," Nina said. "I need my weapon. I think I can get to it in the linen closet."

"No. No time."

He could tell she wanted to argue, but she clamped her mouth shut and silently glared at him in the muted moonlight. Then she called "Come" to Sam.

"Okay then," Thomas said, glad for another small victory. "On three, we crouch and run toward my truck." He turned and pulled his coat over her head. "Keep that on, okay?" The coat's suede skin and shearling lining might shield her from the shooter's aim if she kept running.

"Okay," she said in a reluctant whisper, followed by, "Thomas, thank you."

"Don't thank me yet," he said. Then he shoved against the door and heard the potting table groaning. Thomas grunted and pushed his way through, ignoring the spattering of shots all around them. Both the trash can and the heavy potting table actually served as deflectors.

Nina hurried along behind him, Sam bringing up the rear in silence. The next shot tore a hole in the tin carport roof. Thomas shoved her ahead of him, behind his truck. "Get underneath," he said, urging her to crawl between the big tires.

"Sam, come," she called again. The K-9 got on his belly and did as he'd been trained to do.

Soon, they were safe under the truck's heavy armor.

Thomas lay on his belly, his chest and head lifted, and listened for the footsteps he knew would be coming. It didn't take long.

"I'll try to sneak around," he whispered against Nina's sweet-smelling hair.

The crunch and cracking of boots hitting snow and dirt stopped him. Too late.

Nina pointed to the left.

Thomas nodded. If he could take aim, he could at least maim the intruder.

The man inched within a few feet from them in a matter of seconds. Nina pointed to Sam. Thomas nodded. What better way to take the man down and keep him alive to talk?

Nina raised herself up, about to sound the attack command, when they heard sirens on the road.

The man turned and took off running. Nina shouted, "Attack!"

Sam bolted from under the truck and went into the woods, following the scent of the stranger. Nina pushed away Thomas's coat and started to follow, but he pulled her back. "Wait for backup."

"Give me your weapon," she shouted. Snow was falling all around them now, and her house was full of bullet holes and scattershot.

Thomas shook his head, glad when Max West stalked toward them and asked, "Agent Atkins, are you all right?"

"Yes, sir," Nina answered. Then she launched into a full report, Sam's fierce barking making her fidget. "I need to pursue the suspect, sir."

Max put his hand on her arm. "We've got it covered. Why don't you let the EMTs check out your injuries?"

"I don't have any injuries," she retorted, anger marking each word.

"Yes, you do," Thomas said, taking her by the arm.

She was bleeding from her left shoulder.

SIX

"I'm fine," Nina kept telling everyone. "It's a flesh wound." Sam now stood at attention near where she sat in the back of the open ambulance, with a heavy blanket around her and a big bandage wrapped around her upper left arm. "I'll be okay. I just want to go to bed and sleep for twelve hours."

"Not in this house," Thomas told her. "You're coming to the inn with me."

Nina shook her head. "I want to stay here."

"No," Max said from behind Thomas. "It's either the inn or the bunk room at headquarters. Or I'll take you out to the ranch."

Nina let out a groan of frustration. Three windows shot into rubble and gunshot holes in the side and front doors. The landlord would not be happy, but at least she had renter's insurance. Filing that report would be such fun.

"I'll probably have to move, anyway," she said, with another huff of frustration.

Agent Zeke Morrow strolled up with his Australian shepherd, Cheetah. "Penny has your room ready. We have plenty of dog food and whatever else you might need."

"Isn't that inn getting kind of crowded?" Nina retorted, glaring at Thomas.

"Always room for one more," Zeke replied, his dark eyes solemn and sure. "And I have a temporary apartment not far from there while the house we bought is being renovated, so you're covered if anyone tries to mess with you again."

"I can take care of myself," she said with a weak whine.

"We know," all three men said in weary unison.

Then the SAC leaned over her. "Look, Nina. You're a good agent, but you have a target on your back. Do you really want to sleep here tonight?"

Nina glanced from her shattered little cottage to the man who'd been by her side the whole time. Thomas gave her an understanding glance and waited for her response.

"No," she said, tossing off the blanket. "What I want is to find whoever is behind this. He got away again."

"He had a car right around the corner near the stream that runs along this property. The land on the other side of the stream is fenced and private, but we're working on locating the owner. Sam tracked the shooter to the water and took a bite out of the long trench coat he left behind."

"A DNA petri dish, I hope," Nina said, gaining hope.

"Already on its way to the lab," Thomas replied. "Now, let's go find you some clothes so you can get that sleep you need."

He reached out to help her out of the ambulance. Nina winced when she tried to move her left arm. She'd have a nice bruise just below her shoulder. The bullet had hit her in a bony area, leaving a deep gash that would hold a permanent scar.

"Are you sure you don't need to go to the ER?" Thomas asked, his voice low.

"No. Just a little sore, is all."

"Do you have the pain pills the EMT gave you?"

"Yes," she said. But she didn't intend to take them.

"Okay, I'll drive you to the inn."

"I can take my vehicle."

"You can get your SUV tomorrow once the crime scene techs are done here. Tonight, I'm driving you."

Too tired to argue, she followed him into the shot-up house, past the little tree, which was now toppled over on the floor, its lights and ornaments shattered and crushed. Nina bit her lip, then grabbed her go-bag and her weapon, and allowed him to guide her to his big truck. When he opened the passenger side door, there was a moment when she thought the man was actually going to pick her up and put her inside. But he only stared into her eyes, the storm clouds in his gaze telling her that he was loaded for bear on finding Russo.

Nina tried to hop up onto the seat, but winced in pain.

"I got you," Thomas said, not lifting her, but assisting her with a strong hand that held her with such a sweet strength, Nina's composure almost melted. She got settled and then stared out the window at the yellow crime scene tape now holding her house together.

Thomas got in the truck and put on a cowboy hat. Just like some western hero.

When she looked at the road, news crews were swarming all around, but the FBI team and the local police held them back from her house and yard.

"They'll keep digging," she said. "They might scare Russo away. I hope the reporters don't find Kelly and lead him right to her."

"Kelly is fine. We checked on her at the hospital. They've moved her to a more secure area and Tim Ramsey and his K-9 partner, Frodo, are guarding her, along with the sheriff's deputy."

Breathing a little sigh of relief, since Tim was good at his job and very capable, she kept staring ahead. "Thomas, Russo's getting sloppy. He wants both of us dead, but…this doesn't seem like a hired killer's MO."

"Agreed," Thomas replied, as he pulled the big truck up close to the inn's carriage drive. "While you rest here, we're going to do more digging. Hopefully, we can figure out who the other two victims were. Someone knows something. I might have to make a trip to Helena and ask around about Kelly's life there."

"I'm going with you if you do," she said, determination adding punch to the words.

"No."

"Yes, Thomas. Yes. You said this is my investigation, that I can do the job. So let me. Either help me or get out of my way."

"Nina," he said, turning toward her in the seat. "This man is dangerous."

"I think I've figured that out, since I witnessed him trying to kill a young girl, and especially when I found the bodies he possibly left nearby. He's tried to kill me twice now, so I get it, Thomas. My job is to get to him before he can kill one of us or Kelly Denton. So if you go to Helena to investigate, I'm going with you. And there will be no discussion on that matter."

Thomas didn't argue with her, but Nina had a feeling there would be more discussions between them.

The next morning, Nina woke up and realized where she was and why she'd spent the night in this beautiful room at the Wild Iris Inn. Sam woofed a greeting and stared at his food bowl with doleful eyes.

Her partner never complained. He'd hold off on eating and relieving himself in order to protect her or anyone else. Glancing at the clock, she noted it was six in the morning. She was usually up and ready to go by this time. When she lifted her arm, her wound reminded her that she'd had a close call the night before.

A knock on the door caused her to bolt straight up, sending pain shooting through her body. Sam stood at attention, but didn't seem too worried. A friendly.

"Just a minute," she said, grabbing a robe she'd tossed into her bag last night to put over her T-shirt and plaid pajama bottoms.

Nina opened the door, expecting Thomas to be standing there. But Penny Potter greeted her with a smile, her dark eyes full of concern. "I have strict orders to keep you out of trouble."

Nina laughed but shook her head. "Let me guess. Thomas Grant?"

"Him, and Max West, too. Both very formidable when they need to be."

"They wouldn't treat a man that way."

Penny put down the tray she carried and stared over at Nina. "You're wrong there. When Zeke lost his brother, it was rough for all of us. You've no doubt heard that Jake was the father of my son, Kevin. I fell in love with his half brother, Zeke. We both had a lot of guilt to deal with." She poured coffee and motioned for Nina to sit at the little wooden bistro-style table by the big bay window. "Max told Zeke to take some time off. Ordered it, actually. And he told both of us to talk to counselors and to make sure Kevin got help, too."

Feeling contrite, Nina nodded. "I'm aware of some of that, yes. Zeke was in a lot of pain."

"Yes, but Max went with us to bury Jake in Utah. He didn't have to do that, but he did. He's a good man who guards his team members like he'd guard anyone else, except with his team he not only guards them, he makes sure they are safe and healthy so they can be the best at the dangerous jobs they do."

Nina took a sip of coffee and stared at the blueberry bagel covered with cream cheese on the pretty floral china. "I'm sorry. I just fought against so many condescending colleagues early in my career that I have to remind myself Max is not that way. He expects the best of us, and I've tried to give that, but right now I'm under pressure. If I fail at this case, I fail all of us."

Penny tossed back her long golden-brown hair and smiled. "You won't fail, but you do need to rest. Zeke told me you've been at this for days now."

"Yes," she admitted. "It did feel good to actually sleep last night." Tearing off some of the bagel, she asked, "So where is the notorious Thomas Grant this morning?"

Probably out getting the jump on her.

"He's at headquarters. Said he had to clear something with Max."

"Really?" Nina wished she knew what that something was. He wouldn't demand they remove her from this investigation, would he? Last night, they'd agreed they were in this together.

Penny leaned close, her smile full of understanding. "I'm talking out of school here, but I don't think you have anything to worry about. The man likes you, a lot. Why else would he have guarded your door all night?"

Thomas parked in the covered garage at the back of the inn's property. Dog-tired and needing a shower, he strolled up to the sunporch that covered the entire back of the big, Victorian-style house.

"Well, you've been a very busy man."

Nina sat there, dressed in jeans and a long cardigan sweater over a white blouse, her hair falling in spiky strands around her chin and neck. Sam lay at her feet, doing his job even if he looked deceptively docile.

"I have at that," Thomas admitted. Sinking down in a cushioned wicker rocking chair, he crossed his ankles and took a long breath. "And I'm exhausted."

"Maybe you should stop sleeping in a chair in front of the door to my room."

"I like sleeping in chairs. Builds character." Then he made a face. "But my back is not happy."

"I'm refreshed and anxious to get back to work," she retorted, a bad attitude all over each syllable. "My arm is sore, but workable."

"That's good," he replied, taking his time because she was so amazing when she was in a snit.

Her eyes flashed a dark gold, her foot tapping against the porch floor.

"So, how was your day?" she said with a fake smile. "Mine was really boring."

"My day was productive," he said, wishing he could just catch his man and get away from these strange feelings clawing at his heart. "Are you going to let me explain or would you rather have a hissy fit and get it over with first?"

She got up and crossed her arms over her chest, her eyes shooting sparks. "Explain, Thomas. Now."

"I spent most of today clearing things for *us* to go to Helena together."

Her eyes went wide. "Us? I figured you'd take off without me."

"I did consider that…but I'm not completely stupid. *I* figured you'd hightail it after me."

"You'd be right on that."

He nodded. "I promised Max West I would protect you with my life, then I talked to Dylan O'Leary and some of the other techs and found out that the other two girls have been ID'd and they were both also from Helena."

She forgot to be mad and sank like a rock on the chair next to his. "Wow."

"Yeah, but the *wow* gets even more wowee. They all worked at the state capitol in Helena as interns while they attended school nearby."

Another *wow* and he had her listening.

"One girl disappeared earlier this year and the other one about three months ago. The bodies we found have definitely been identified as these two. No doubt there. I have pictures of all three of them now."

"And...can we prove Russo killed them?"

"Based on particles and hair follicles found on the trench coat, and some fibers and epidermis particles we found on Kelly's coat and underneath her nails, we can prove Russo was with her that night. The lab is comparing fibers they discovered on the remains of the girls, too, but they haven't come up with a match yet."

"Russo," she said, standing up again. "So he's not as meticulous as we thought, and we have him for shooting Kelly Denton. When do we leave?"

"First thing tomorrow," Thomas replied. Then he pulled something out of his coat pocket and handed it to her.

"The hot chocolate mix?" she said, her eyes widening, both hands holding tight to the glass jar.

"For tonight." He gave her a Thomas Special grin and winked. "I'm going to take a shower. I hope Penny planned something good for dinner. I'm starving."

Nina watched as he walked inside. Then she stared at the mixture of sugar, cinnamon, powdered chocolate and powdered milk in her hand. He'd found it and saved it for her. Which meant he'd been back to her house today.

A wonderful gesture that touched her heart. But she had to wonder if he'd found something else there that had him ready to do battle on her behalf.

Nina intended to find out if Thomas knew more than he was telling her. And if she had to do it over hot chocolate, she would.

SEVEN

"How did you find this place?" Nina asked the next day, after they'd driven the close to four hours to Helena.

Helena was a bustling city that moved on in spite of snow on the ground and Christmas shoppers hurrying here and there. But Thomas had driven straight through without so much as a grunt of impatience.

The tiny condo building held maybe twelve units and was centrally located, near the state capitol. Clean and cozy, their unit consisted of an open den and kitchen with a stunning fireplace and a short hall to two bedrooms, each with its own bath and a slight view of the capitol building.

"We use it…sometimes."

Sam, always curious, sniffed and stared, checking the place out. The big dog gave Nina a questioning glance. Always ready to roll.

But for the moment, Nina was focusing on the man standing across from her.

"Oh, I see." How could she forget one of the main aspects of his job—moving witnesses here and there to keep them safe until they could either obtain a new identity and location, or at least testify and put someone evil away? "So you're been here before?"

"Once or twice."

And he couldn't tell her anything more. Nina wondered what kind of burdens this man carried inside that big heart.

"It's nice."

"And secure," he added. "The entry gate is state-of-the-art and the security system is high tech, too. Plus a lot of the people who live here are either law enforcement or work at the capitol."

Nina dropped her gear and put her hands on her hips, her left arm still smarting from the gunshot wound. "So we start with the capitol?"

"Yes," he said, his expression stern while he lifted curtains and tugged on windows. He was checking the place for vulnerability. The man was a stickler for protocol, but then she was, too. "We'll have to be cautious. Can't go about accusing our state leaders without a good reason."

"No, not after what you told me last night and on the ride here."

They *had* shared cups of hot chocolate last night, after a hearty dinner of baked chicken with wild rice. Penny was a much more discreet innkeeper than her boss, Claire, had ever been. She'd left them to eat and then sent them out on the sunporch, where a woodstove kept things toasty.

Nina had immediately questioned Thomas last night about why he'd gone back to her house. He'd admitted he wanted to see it in the light of day and possibly find something they could use as evidence. The crime scene techs had already compared the shell casings they'd found there to the ones they'd retrieved in the parking garage the night Nina and Thomas had been shot at.

A match that indicated the same shotgun could have been used in both.

"So…that's it. The one thing you were holding back on," she said.

"Not holding back. Just trying to figure some things out."

"Because it doesn't add up, right?"

It was much harder to get in a good shot with a shotgun unless the gunman was at close range, like last night. But at close range, a shotgun could do a lot more damage to either an object or a human. Russo would be the type to take pleasure in blowing someone to pieces. But Russo wouldn't be messing around like this. He'd wait and find the perfect cover and then he'd target his prey and end things, quickly and thoroughly, probably with a high-powered rifle or a silencer gun like the one Nina had seen the other night.

None of this made any sense.

"That means the shooter was close to us the other night in the garage," Nina said to Thomas. "But a pro would have used a rifle with a scope."

"From a safe distance away," Thomas replied, showing her they'd come to the same conclusion. "It would have been quick and clean."

Now she had to wonder if he knew something about the weapon or the shooter that she'd missed. But they both agreed that something was off, at least.

"He probably didn't use a shotgun on the girls," she said now. "He used a silencer when he targeted Kelly Denton, but he was running away and didn't get in a good shot."

Thomas rubbed the back of his neck. "The shotgun is sending a message. I don't know what that means yet, but I hope we'll find out something here."

"Maybe he was just shooting that night to scare us."

"Or maim one of us for life, if not worse."

Nina went still. "Or...there's someone else involved. Someone who's not a professional assassin."

"Bingo."

Thomas opened the refrigerator and then turned to stare at her across the white marble countertop. "I made some calls to the Helena police before we left this morning. They are, of course, aware of the missing girls."

"What else did you find out?" Nina asked, thinking she'd reprimand him later for not telling her until now. "Don't try to protect me, Thomas. I need to know.'

He finally looked her square in the eyes. "They all worked at one time for Senator Slaton."

Nina took in a breath. "What are you saying?"

"I don't know," he replied, doubt in his solemn gaze. "I don't want to speculate."

"So you didn't think to run this by me immediately?"

"Nina, Russo is after you, too, and you've got a wound to prove it. I didn't want to…"

"Scare me? Not telling me scares me even more. The girls are connected and…we might have more than one suspect."

"I didn't want to worry you," he said, the statement full of stubbornness. Then he held up his hand to ward off her glare of aggravation. "If a state senator is involved, you know what that could mean."

"Yes," she retorted, not sure whether to appreciate him or shout at him. "It could mean someone's targeting his staff. Or it could mean something entirely different. If he is involved, it means I'm going to take down a state senator."

"That's it right there," he replied, his eyes going so serious he did begin to scare her. "You're so good at your job you're forgetting to be cautious."

"How can I *not* be cautious when a killer is on my trail, Thomas? I've been as cautious as possible, considering I have a giant Texas shadow hanging over my head. And now we think this goes even deeper. We don't know how the senator could be involved. Maybe he's a victim or he could be a criminal. This isn't about being cautious. This is about doing the jobs we're both trained to do. Together, whether we like it or not."

"I like it," he said in a quick clipped tone. "The together part, I mean."

Nina's breath left her body, but her heart chased after it, needing to get away from that stormy-eyed stare.

"I like *you*," he continued. "I'm going to protect *you*. We need to be clear on that."

Sam shot her a hard, stoic glance. As if the dog was agreeing with the deputy marshal. Great, they were ganging up on her.

She'd almost left Sam behind, because they planned to stay under the radar and a K-9 dog would bring attention to them immediately. But now she was glad she had her faithful partner here to shield her from Thomas Grant. Not in a hostile, take-down way, but in a protect-my-heart-please way.

Swallowing her pride and that burst of warmth and security his nearness gave her, she pushed at her hair and said, "Tell me what the locals gave you so we can get to work and get this over with."

So she obviously didn't like working with *him*.

And she sure didn't like his trying to protect her.

She wanted this done and over so she could be rid of him.

Fair enough then.

Thomas sat down and stared up at her. "Why don't I take you to lunch and we'll talk?"

"We'll talk here," she said, digging in her heels. Sam sank down at her feet.

Thomas motioned to the chair across from him. After she sat, he said, "The locals did all they could to search for each girl. The cases remain active and they're now aware that we've identified the bodies. They want to know everything we know and they're willing to let us go over their files and compare notes."

"Let's get busy," she said, standing to straighten her clothes. "And we need to talk to Senator Slaton."

Today, she wore a black suit and sensible heels so she'd blend in with government workers. Since he'd rarely seen her dressed up, Thomas acknowledged to himself how pretty she looked, no matter what she wore. But he also reminded himself that her job came first. He'd always felt the same, until now.

Nina didn't have a clue what he was thinking. She was too busy calling the state senator's office.

"He's away on a hunting vacation," she said, turning back to Thomas. "How convenient."

"I wonder what he's hunting?" Thomas replied.

"Yeah, me, too," Nina said, prancing toward the door. "But while the senator's away, we can see what other people have to say."

"And she's a poet."

So they headed to police headquarters, careful to make sure they weren't being followed or watched, and entered the back way. Over the next few hours, they scrolled through reports and files and studied what little evidence had been stored.

"We found one cell phone," a detective told them. "Had the lab analyze it and talked to most of her contacts, but based on some text messages from last December, all we found significant was regarding a party. A very private party."

About three weeks later, the girl went missing.

And they'd never found out where the party took place, since at the time, her friends had claimed they didn't know. A wall of silence, according to one detective. They hadn't realized the two missing girls were connected until now, so of course they needed updates.

"Who did she meet at that party?" Nina asked Thomas now, her eyes scanning the file she'd just opened. "Here's a list of her phone contacts, but there's no information to go on with the names. Maybe we should dig deeper into her phone records or interview some of these contacts."

"I'm sure the locals did that already," Thomas replied, "but it never hurts to go back over things, especially now that we know who we could be dealing with. As for the party, maybe it being so secretive had something to do with her disappearance."

"You mean, like maybe someone on the senator's staff made her disappear?"

"Yeah, like that," Thomas replied with a dead-pan look. "Let's keep to the plan and start there first."

"Good idea." Nina called out to where Sam had been waiting patiently while they studied files. He'd get to visit the Helena K-9 kennels while they did some footwork

But after an hour or so of getting the runaround at the senator's office and being passed from a secretary to an aide and then hitting brick walls, they left without any relevant information.

"On to the friends list," Nina said.

They started with Mya Gregory, since she'd disappeared first.

Her mother greeted them with red-rimmed eyes and a frail stare. Thomas noticed she looked physically ill.

"We're so sorry for your loss," he said, after Nina had explained why they were there. Mrs. Gregory showed them into a modestly decorated den.

"Thank you," she said, taking her time as she sank down in a chair near a table laden with medical bottles and supplies. Noticing their expressions, she said, "I'm dying of cancer. I'm only talking to you today because… I hope they find out who did this before I die. I'm not afraid to go. I'm ready to see Mya again. But I want justice for my sweet girl, especially now that I know she's never coming back."

Nina leaned forward. "Can you tell us what happened and if you have any information that can help us?"

Mrs. Gregory launched into a detailed timeline. Her husband and she had divorced years ago, but she'd had a steady job and Mya had scholarships and student loans to pay off. "When she got the news about interning at the capitol, she was so happy. She studied political science and took all kinds of government-related classes. She loved being around our state leaders, but then…something went wrong last December. She attended some fancy Christmas party with her friends, and after that she seemed so sad and worried. She wouldn't talk about it, but her whole demeanor changed. She became anxious and secretive."

"And then she went missing," Nina finished, sympathy in her eyes.

"Yes, in early January, right after the spring semester started back up." Mrs. Gregory coughed and Thomas handed her a glass of water from the table. "I tried everything, you know. Talked to the police, gave them all the information I could think of, but… I was shut down at every angle." She sipped the water. "At least now I can bury my baby."

Then she said something that brought Thomas

and Nina to full attention. "And maybe now, the threats will stop."

"Threats!"

Nina and Thomas had found a quiet corner café near the condo to have an early dinner. He looked over at her now, taking in the irate expression that only made her more beautiful. "Yeah, imagine that. But in spite of the threats, Mya's mother was smart. She did a pretty good job of digging around in a high-powered world."

Mrs. Gregory had found several of Mya's friends and asked them about the party and why her daughter had seemed so unhappy and distraught after she'd gone to it. None of them could tell her much.

"But someone came to her house and told her to stop digging," Nina replied, checking out the window to where they'd left Sam in the unmarked SUV they'd rented, in sight and with a window cracked open to the chilly night.

"And left threatening messages on her phone."

"The woman is so scared she won't even tell us who it was."

"That's because she wants to live long enough to bury Mya," Thomas reminded her, wishing he could do more for that poor woman and for the upset one sitting across from him.

Nina sank back in the cushioned booth where big clear windows on both sides gave them a view outside and where they could see the whole narrow restaurant and each entryway. "At least she gave us some names. If we find one person who's willing to talk, maybe we'll get to the bottom of this." She took a drink of her sparkling water. "But Thomas, we both know the signs. Someone must have been threatening Mya, too. That means she and the other girl saw something at that party that really shook them up. Kelly Denton has to know what that was, but she's too scared to tell us. Or maybe she's scared because she's the victim."

"Something happened that they couldn't forget," Thomas added. "Something that was so bad, two of them died because of it. And the one left isn't talking."

Nina's head came up. "Thomas, don't you think it strange that Mya's contact list didn't include Kelly and the other girl?"

"They don't necessarily have to know each other," he said, his gut suddenly tightening. "It could be that they purposely avoided each other— a protective kind of thing." Checking out the window he added, "But if they were all interns at the same time and were all at that party together, they could have formed a pact or something. Or they could have a piece of incriminating evidence."

"I don't know if I can eat," Nina said, staring down at her baked chicken and vegetables. "This smacks of some sort of high-level cover-up."

"You didn't have lunch," Thomas pointed out,

unable to stop the feelings of concern. "How's your wound?"

"It's burning like a brand, but I'm okay."

"Try your veggies," he coaxed. "I need you strong and sharp." When that didn't work, he took her hand. "Remember, you saved Kelly's life. I'm going to keep you safe."

She glared at him for a few tense seconds. "I'm not worried about being safe right now, but thanks. I guess I'm just going to have to go with the cowboy-to-the-rescue thing, right?"

"Might be best," he said, wishing she'd see that he wanted to keep her away from this evil. Not just because she was a good officer and needed in Billings, not only because she was a witness to a crime and needed his protection, but also because he really liked being around her and...hoped that maybe one day they could have a quiet meal together with no mayhem involved. "I'm not going to change," he added. "My mama raised me right."

Nina laughed at that. "Yes, she sure did."

Then he put down his water glass and said, "Actually, that's not true. Like I told you, she left me behind after my parents divorced. And my dad didn't know how to deal with me, so I had a lot of mamas, but none of them were really mine to claim."

Nina's expression softened. "Like I said the other night, if we survive this, I'm taking you to my parents' house for Christmas."

"I can't argue with that, since I aim to survive and keep you alive, too."

"As long as we keep doing this together and you understand I don't need a babysitter, we'll be fine."

"I don't want to be your babysitter," he replied, shaking his head. "I need your expertise and I want us to be equal partners. But I'm going to watch after you, Nina."

She opened her mouth to deliver what surely would be a protest and then changed her frown into a little smile. "Okay, Thomas. We'll go with that for now."

"Eat your veggies," he said again, laughing at her in spite of the many questions he had about those three girls.

EIGHT

Nina couldn't believe how Thomas had helped her relax. He'd told her stories of past cases, leaving out names and the bad parts. Told her about his childhood of moving around and never having a real home. Then he got her talking about her brothers and how they'd picked on her without mercy and taught her to be tough.

"I can see that," he said, his gaze washing over her face in a not-so-businesslike way.

His gentle eyes held something that made her blush and wonder what was happening between them.

When they settled on her lips, Nina took a deep breath and pushed her plate away. "It's getting late."

"Yeah, I guess it is."

His statement held so much more than just weary agreement.

He shot her one last glance that held longing and regret, and then his phone buzzed, causing them to part like two guilty teens.

"Thomas Grant," he said into his cell, his gaze still on Nina. But the tender expression on his face changed. "I see. Can we meet and talk about this?"

Nina listened intently and saw a flare of awareness in his eyes. "Well, thank you for the information."

He ended the call and let out a long sigh. "That

was one of the friends we tried to contact. Remember Jack Creighton? We talked to him on the phone and he agreed to speak to us in person?"

"Yes," she said. "The last one on our list, out from the city. He knew Mya, right? But he didn't open the door when we got to his house."

"He obviously found the card I stuck in the mailbox," Thomas stated. "And had a change of heart."

"Does he want to see us now?"

"No. He quickly gave me a rundown and then hung up."

"And?"

"He said we needed to find Slaton's son Allen. He implied the senator has kept his misdeeds under wraps for too long."

Nina put her hands on the table and pushed herself up. "Three scared girls and one senator's son. What happened at that party, Thomas?"

"Probably something we don't want to hear about," he replied. Throwing enough money on the table to cover the meal and tip, he took her by the hand and they hurried out of the restaurant.

"I'll report to Dylan," she said, pulling out her phone. "He can do some more research."

Thomas hit the key fob and the SUV's locks clicked open. He was right behind her as they walked across the street. But she heard a thump and a grunt before they reached the vehicle. Whirling, she spotted Thomas hitting the hard pavement. Nina jumped back just as a man charged toward her and knocked her purse to the ground. She went into action and gave the attacker a swift kick in the stomach, and then slugged him with a right hook before she jabbed him with her elbow, screaming at the top of her lungs the whole time.

Inside the SUV, Sam went wild, barking and dancing in the seat. If she could get to the door...

But the man overpowered her and shoved her hard against the big vehicle, his hands reaching for her throat. Nina gasped and prepared to do battle, but before she could trip him up and get to where her weapon remained hidden in her dropped purse, a big swoosh of air hit her and her attacker went down.

Thomas body-slammed the guy, knocking him into the street. Nina breathed deep and rushed to get her gun. The man fell a few feet away, but got up and took off running toward a dark alley, Sam's barks echoing after him. Thomas, still weak, started to follow, but when people came charging out of the restaurant, he turned and yelled to them to get back inside.

Then he passed out and fell to the ground again.

Thomas woke up with a jolt and blinked. When he saw Nina hovering over him, he grabbed her hand. "Are you all right?"

Nina gently pulled his hands away. "I'm fine. Lie back. We're almost to the hospital."

Straining to see, Thomas realized they were in an ambulance. "No, I'm fine. I'm supposed to take care of you."

And he'd failed.

"Thomas, listen to me," she said, using an authoritative voice. "You got hit over the head with a baseball bat. You probably have a concussion."

"I said I'm fine," he lied. In fact, his skull was hammering like a construction crew way behind on the job. "Turn this bus around."

"No. It's my turn to watch over you, you big oaf."

Squinting at her to make sure she was in one piece, he glanced at her hand on his arm. There was a lot of strength in that firm grip. "Did you just call me an oaf?"

"Yes, and I'll call you worse if you move again. The locals are searching for our assailant and Sam is safe with one of their handlers. The man left the bat, but he was wearing gloves, so no good prints to speak of. Witnesses only saw an average-size man wearing a heavy black dress coat and a dark hat pulled low. I saw his face, but he had on dark glasses. I don't think I could identify him."

Thomas blinked again, trying to keep up. Her chatter was nervous and nerve-racking. "If you'll be quiet, I'll lie still," he finally said. "Since you have everything under control."

"Good idea," she replied. "We're at the ER, so hang on."

Thomas fell back and closed his eyes, the image of the attacker going for Nina's throat making a loop inside his head that angered him to no end.

He'd humor her for now...but he wasn't going to spend the night in the hospital.

Thankfully, he convinced the ER doctor of that, too. Soon, they were in a patrol car, being taken back to their vehicle, where they were reunited with Sam. Nina got the rottweiler settled in the back and put Thomas in the passenger seat and hopped up to drive, adjusting the seat from tall to short to accommodate.

"Am I safe with you?" he asked, trying to relieve some of the tension.

"Always," she said. Then she turned to him. "Are you sure you're okay to go back to the condo?"

"Yes. You can keep me awake with your annoying, bossy chatter."

"I'll be glad to, since you looked after me when I got grazed with that bullet."

He'd seen her arm earlier. In her efforts to take down the attacker, she'd caused her wound to start bleeding again. She now wore a fresh bandage under the red stains on her white blouse.

Gritting his teeth, Thomas squelched the frustration of not being able to help her when she'd needed him, and promised himself that wouldn't happen again.

After scanning the area where they parked close to the front door, she had him inside and pointed him toward the couch. Then she checked the backside and small patio, too. "Nothing out of the ordinary, but why do I feel as if we're being watched?"

"Shut the door and bolt it, Nina."

She did that and then set the alarm. Sam cleared the rooms while Thomas fell into a pile on the couch.

She scooted around in the tiny kitchen and came to sit down beside him. "Hot tea," she said, shoving a mug at him. "Drink it."

"I don't like hot tea."

"It's herbal, so it won't mess with your head. Drink it."

"*You're* messing with my head," he retorted. "Nina, maybe it's the knocking I took, but you look so beautiful."

"You definitely have a concussion." She put the tea down and stared at him. "Thomas, you scared me."

"I was trying to save you, but you saved yourself and me."

"Are you going to pout about that? You've saved me a couple of times already, so you're still ahead."

He took her hand, thinking because he was

weak and woozy he'd milk this for all it was worth. "I'm not pouting. In fact, while we're sitting here doing nothing, you can do that research on what Jack Creighton told us with such cryptic details. That is, when you're not waiting on me hand and foot."

Even if he couldn't see straight right now, he could at least enjoy watching her.

"I can do that," she said, staring down at his hand over hers. "Right after you take two pain pills. You can rest, but I'm supposed to wake you every few hours."

He liked that idea. But not the medicine. "I don't need pain pills."

"Yes, you do. You know how it works with a slight concussion, I'm sure."

"I do and that's why I don't need pain pills. I have a hard head." Then he motioned toward her arm. "Same way you have tough skin."

"Take your medicine and I'll share what I find out on Jack Creighton."

"You don't play fair."

"All's fair in love and crime."

She called Dylan, knowing he wouldn't mind the late hour. While she waited to see what he could find, she searched for information on Jack Creighton and found a wealth of photos on his social media profile going back well over a year or so.

She checked on Thomas. He was dozing. She'd wake him in a few minutes. Something on her laptop screen caught her attention.

Jack Creighton in a picture with Allen Slaton. A school photo with their names listed. They'd played soccer and football together, the usual prep school activities.

But these photos showed they were friends. Were they still friends? Had Jack called to help them or get them off the trail?

After scrolling through a few more posts and discovering information that would help their case she turned to wake up Thomas.

The man lay there watching her, his eyes open and lucid. Too lucid.

"I like the way you bite your lower lip when you're researching," he said, his voice gravelly with sleep.

"I can see you're going to live," she retorted with a drip of sarcasm to hide the treacherous tremor of her pulse. "Do you want to keep lying there with that flirty look on your face, or do you want to know what Dylan and I have found?"

"I don't know," he said, slowly raising himself with a grimace. "I sure enjoy flirting with you even though it's not very professional." Then he chuckled. "You know, if you closed that laptop, you'd be off duty. Then we wouldn't have to follow the rules."

She stood and leaned over him, thinking she

might actually flirt back, then shook her head and sat down on the couch. "Easy, cowboy. When you hear what I found, you'll forget all about me."

"No, I won't," he said, rubbing a hand over his beautifully tousled hair. "Work first. Then we can get back to the good stuff."

For the first time in her career, Nina wished work didn't have to come first. Which only proved it should, in spite of the Texas-bred distraction sitting next to her.

"I found out about the party," she said, figuring that would get his mind back on the job.

It did. He frowned at her, obviously going on full alert. "Tell me everything." Then he glanced toward the kitchen. "I'm kind of hungry, so I'll eat while you report."

"I'll make you a sandwich while I talk," she replied, thinking this domestication stuff sure was cozy. And deciding his grocery bill must be huge.

But she went on with her report. While she found the ham and cheese and pickles and bread they'd bought earlier, she said, "The party was held last year, a week before Christmas, at a private club on the other side of town. A chateau owned by a corporation. A fraternity and a sorority put it together. And guess who attended?"

Thomas took the sandwich she'd slapped together and cut in half. "Let me see—our three girls and this Jack dude and... Allen Slaton?"

"Yes, all of the above, along with about thirty

others," she said with a solemn stare. "Dylan located the other girl's father. Her mother passed away a few years ago, but Kristen Banks's dad is still here in Helena. We can try to contact him first thing tomorrow."

"Sounds like a plan," Thomas said, admiration in his eyes. "This sandwich is great."

"It's just bread and ham, cheese and mustard, Thomas."

"But you cooked for me. And added pickles."

"Don't get used to that."

He finished his sandwich, then went to the bathroom to freshen up. She pulled out a bag of cookies he'd nabbed at the nearby grocery store, thinking she needed something to nibble on instead of his enticing lips. When he came back they ate cookies, drank coffee and talked about the investigation for a few minutes, developing a solid plan for the next day. Then he tugged her down onto the couch.

"I'm ready to do some serious flirting," he announced.

Nina's heart did a somersault. "I haven't flirted in so long I'm not sure how to respond."

Sam yawned from his spot on the rug by the window.

"Just be you," Thomas said, and then he laughed and pulled her close. "We're a good team, Nina. Thank you for saving yourself tonight and for taking care of me."

"My job," she said, her voice turning mushy. "But this… Thomas… I'm not so good at this."

He leaned close, his incredible eyes holding her gaze. "We'll learn together, and once this is all over…we'll be pros in the relationship department, too."

Then he kissed her, a soft warm whisper on her lips that shot a sizzle all the way to her heart. Pulling back just a breath, he said, "Meantime, you know what they say. Practice makes perfect."

Nina kissed him again for good measure.

NINE

Jeffrey Banks looked as haggard and tired as Mya Gregory's mother, but he wasn't sick, physically. The man was suffering from grief. At first he was wary, but after they showed him their badges and explained why they needed to talk to him, he told them about how he'd raised Kristen alone after his wife died.

"She wanted to be a nurse like her mom but she also liked politics so she wound up working for Senator Slaton—just a temporary part-time thing. She had one more year of college when she...just disappeared."

"I'm so sorry," Nina said. "We want to find justice for these girls."

"So now that she's dead, everyone comes running," he said on a grim note while they stood in the hallway of his modest, two-story home. "Nobody seemed to care before."

"We care," Nina said, wishing she could ease his pain. "That's why we're here. We want to find the people who did this."

"I already talked to that other detective about a week ago," Mr. Banks said, rubbing his salt-and-pepper beard. "He wanted to go through her things, but I told him not without a search warrant. And I had my shotgun in his face to prove it."

Nina glanced at Thomas, both of them taking

note of the shotgun comment. "Who was this detective? Did he give you a name?"

"No. He looked mighty young. Clean-cut. I don't believe he was any kind of law officer. You know how you get a bad vibe with people? I never saw a badge and he never actually told me his name, so we didn't get very far into the conversation. He left when my 12-gauge and I refused to let him in my house."

"Have you traveled anywhere recently?" Thomas asked. "Been on any hunting trips?"

The man looked at him as if he'd gone mad. "No, sir. I rarely get out Helena. I'm a maintenance worker with the highway department. Do you have a warrant to search my house?"

"No." Thomas showed him a picture of Russo. "Is this the man who questioned you?"

"Nawh. Too old and too tall."

"How about this one?" she asked, showing him a picture of Allen Slaton.

"That might be him, yes."

Nina jotted notes. Mya's mother had said someone threatened her over the phone. Could that be the same person who'd tried to get past Mr. Banks? Someone else who was looking for clues? Slaton? Russo would have shot Mr. Banks and searched the house, making it look like a robbery. Not his style to back down. Mr. Banks owned a shotgun, but a lot of people did and Thomas hadn't pushed him on that issue. She ruled out the possibility of his lying. What purpose would the man have to go to Billings and shoot at them?

No, this was looking more and more like the senator or his son. Or maybe both.

Nina took a chance and went down another path. "Did Kristen ever mention anything about a key?"

Mr. Banks looked surprised, his eyebrows rising. "She had lots of keys—to her car, her gym locker, her apartment."

"Did she confide in you?" Thomas asked. "About her life? Did she seem distant, or worried about anything?"

Mr. Banks stood up straight. "My daughter was a good girl. Loved the outdoors. Never met a stranger." Then he looked down at the floor. "But yes, something was eating at her when she came by at Christmas last year. I figured she had boyfriend problems. She quit jogging or taking long walks, and joined a gym, which wasn't like her. She hated gyms."

He shook his head, his eyes watering. "The gym called me about two weeks ago and said she had a locker and that her membership needed to be renewed in a month." He blinked back tears. "I didn't tell them my little girl had been missing for almost a year." Giving in to the tears, he gulped, "Now I have to tell them she won't be coming back at all."

"So she joined this gym after Christmas?" Thomas asked, his tone gentle.

"Yeah. Now that I think about it, I might have that locker key. She left it here last time I saw her. She must have forgotten it."

A buzz moved through Nina's system as she glanced over at Thomas. "Can you find the key?"

"I'll be right back." Mr. Banks pivoted and shuffled to the rear of the house.

"I think we're getting somewhere," Thomas said in a whisper. "If Allen Slaton came here, he must have had a very good reason."

Mr. Banks returned with the key, and instead of handing it over, he told them to follow him to the gym, just down the road. So they did, and Sam went inside with them.

And came up empty.

"Nothing in there," Kristen's father said. "I guess I'll never know why someone had to murder my baby."

He left, not bothering to shut the locker or tell the gym employees that his daughter was deceased.

Sam sniffed, but didn't alert. The locker didn't give them any answers. Had someone beat them here with another key?

"If Kristen was hiding something here, it's gone now," Nina said. "Let's ask around."

No one at the gym could remember Kristen or what might have been in her locker, so no help there. Nina and Thomas left, defeated but still determined.

"We've asked around at the capitol and we've talked to as many contacts as we could," Thomas said, once they were back in the vehicle. Nina was still driving, since his headaches seemed to come and go. "I think we need to get back to Billings."

Nina didn't want to give up, but they couldn't stay here indefinitely, and the locals hadn't found the man who'd attacked them last night. Not yet, anyway.

"I hate to admit defeat but…we keep running into roadblocks, and Senator Slaton is obviously making himself unavailable. Plus we can't seem to locate his son. But Mr. Banks might be able to ID him, so that's good."

"Which means this trip wasn't wasted," Thomas replied, while she headed out into midday traffic. "The senator and his son are now on our suspect list and we know the girls were at that party, along with Allen Slaton and the Creighton boy. We also have reason to believe Kristen Banks might have hidden something in her gym locker, but I don't think she ever worked out in that gym. Maybe we should go back and talk to Jack Creighton again, shake him up enough that he'll tell us everything."

"Someone came after us last night, so that means someone knows we're here and why," Nina reminded him. "I just feel like we're so close."

They made it back to the condo without incident

and Thomas turned to stare at her. "I discovered one more important thing on this trip," he said, leaning close, his sleepy eyes moving over her face. "I really like flirting with you and kissing you."

Nina's blush warmed the truck. "Yeah, there is that."

He moved closer, but her phone buzzed. "Hold that kiss," she said with a smile, her heart going weak. "Atkins," she said into the phone, her eyes still on Thomas.

"Nina, it's Dylan."

"Hey," she said. "I'm putting you on speaker."

"Good, 'cause you'll both want to hear this," he replied. "We just found some information that's kind of significant. The land where you came across Russo and Kelly Denton and found those dead girls, well, it's part of an estate that's owned by Senator Richard Slaton. And we have reason to believe he's at his hunting lodge across the stream from the crime scene and that he's been there for days."

Nina's gaze slammed into Thomas's. "We're getting ready to return there now." Then she added, "And Dylan, make sure security is beefed up at the hospital. He could be coming for Kelly Denton."

She ended the call and they hurried to get their belongings so they could head back to Billings. Thomas's phone rang when they were about to close down the condo.

"What now?" he said, before taking the call. Putting it on speaker as Nina had done, he said, "Thomas Grant."

"Marshal, I remembered something."

Mya's mother.

"What's that, Mrs. Gregory?"

"I found a key and I think it belongs to a safety deposit box or something. I have a rental receipt. Mya must have rented the box for some reason."

Nina's heart hammered with so many mixed emotions she couldn't catch up with herself. The direction this investigation seemed to be headed made her ill with grief for those poor girls, but the relationship between Thomas and her had her on edge in a different way. Now she was worried about something happening to him. Silly, since the man could certainly take care of himself.

Is this how it begins? she wondered as they sped across town to Mrs. Gregory's house. *This burning in the heart, this wanting to do everything within your power to save another person's pain?*

Is this what falling in love feels like?

Pushing at her hair, she glanced over at Thomas. She had met him only days ago and yet she felt such a connection with him, such a sweet security and the confidence that she could trust him with her life. And with her heart.

Oh, no. This couldn't be happening. She couldn't fall for the Texan. He understood her job, but he did the same kind of work. They'd always be in some sort of competition. He could turn out like her brothers and father, always teasing her and making her feel as if she didn't measure up.

But he hasn't done that, she thought. And she knew he wouldn't. Thomas respected her even when he was trying to protect her.

They reached Mrs. Gregory's short driveway, and Nina had to put this new realization on the rear burner while she backed the SUV in for security measures. This could be over soon and Thomas would go back to his world.

And leave her to take care of herself.

They got out, Sam with them, and Nina ordered the dog to guard the front porch. Sam would bark at anyone who approached.

They knocked and Mrs. Gregory opened the door, her eyes wide and red-rimmed. "Thank you for coming," she said, glancing back. "I...hated to bother you, but I had to—to let you know."

Nina glanced at Thomas. Something was off. Sam's ears were lifted and he seemed to be alerting, his gaze on the frail woman.

Nina decided they needed to get inside, fast. Sam must be picking up on the woman's fear.

"What do you have for us?" she asked, once they'd stepped inside. Thomas scanned the tiny living and dining area and sent Nina a subtle nod.

"I went through some of Mya's things. It was hard but... I thought maybe I'd find something important. I found a receipt for what looks like a bank box."

Nina took a pair of tweezers from her coat pocket and held up the receipt Mrs. Gregory had handed her. "Looks like she rented a safety deposit box."

Thomas kept a visual on the rooms, but Nina could tell he was getting antsy. Sam stood just outside the open door and emitted a low growl. Now they were both on edge.

"You mentioned a key," he said to the woman, his gaze moving over the house.

She nodded, tears forming in her eyes, her hands trembling. "Yes, here it is." Taking the key from her pocket, she handed it to Thomas. "I'm sorry."

Nina quickly put it and the receipt in two clear evidence bags she'd had tucked into her pocket. "You have nothing to be sorry about. You're doing the right thing. This might help us figure out what Mya was hiding. What she was so depressed and upset about."

Sam growled low.

Mrs. Gregory shook her head, but before she could speak, a man wearing a dark coat stepped out of the tiny hall bathroom.

"I'd like to know the answer to that myself," he said, his gun trained on all of them. "Mrs. Gregory and I have had such a good visit today. But… I really wanted to see both of you, too, so I *convinced* her to call you. And I especially wanted to take that key…right out of your hands. Before I kill you both."

"Russo," Thomas said, disgust in his voice.

Nina recognized him immediately and went for her weapon, but the gunman pressed his weapon against Mrs. Gregory's skinny back. "We've been waiting for you. I really needed all three of you here. Makes things so much easier."

Behind them, Nina heard another low growl. Sam knew this man, too. "So you'll make it look like we were involved, or that we came here to confront Mrs. Gregory and this frail little woman took both of us down?"

"Something like that," Russo said, his voice polite and quiet. "I'll figure out the details later."

He shoved Mrs. Gregory toward them. "Shut the door so that feral animal doesn't take a bite out of me."

Nina turned toward the doorway, hoping she could sic Sam on the man before he took this any further. Then she heard harsh, ragged laughter, and glanced back to see Mrs. Gregory's somewhat hysterical expression.

The woman whirled toward Russo, her skinny finger jabbing into his chest. "Shoot me first, please," she said with a wave of her other hand. "You can do whatever you want with those two nosy know-it-alls. Just put me out of my misery so I can see my daughter again."

She advanced on Russo, surprising all of them

enough to distract the man. Thomas didn't waste any time. He plunged forward and Mrs. Gregory, suddenly spry, hopped out of the way and watched with a gleeful satisfaction as Thomas knocked Russo back, both men wrestling with the gun Russo still held. Nina got out her weapon and opened the door wide.

"Sam. Attack!"

Sam took a giant leap and nabbed Russo just as Thomas twisted the other man around. Thomas let go and got out of the way, watching with heaving breath as Sam put a bite hold on Russo's left calf. The man screamed and dropped his gun, fighting and tugging, which only made Sam hold on with all his strength.

Thomas kicked Russo's weapon away and then, his own gun trained on the screaming criminal, glanced to where Mrs. Gregory leaned against a table, all her energy spent.

Nina went to the woman and helped her to the couch. "Are you all right?"

"I'm fine now, honey," she said. "We got him, didn't we? We got the man who killed my Mya."

"I think so," Nina replied. "Thank you for what you did."

Mrs. Gregory sank against the sofa, her voice low, her eyes watery. "I had to do what he asked, but wasn't about to let him hurt either of you. I figured if I got you here, together we'd take care of the rest."

TEN

Three hours later, Nina and Thomas were on their way to the bank to open the safety deposit box, a warrant in hand and an urgency in their actions. They now knew the safety deposit box had been rented by Mya Gregory.

"At least Russo is off the streets," Thomas said, his heart still jumpy from finding Russo standing there behind Mrs. Gregory.

The man had worked his way into her house and made her search her daughter's things. Then he'd forced her to call Thomas and Nina, so he could end it all, leaving with what he needed and no witnesses left. But that had backfired on him.

"Yes," Nina replied with a long sigh. "And we have one feisty woman to thank for that."

"A brave woman," Thomas said. "She risked her life to help us and to save us."

"But…she won't make it much longer, Thomas. Once Mya's remains are released for burial, her mother won't be far behind her."

"We'll check on her," he said, meaning it. "She doesn't have anyone, but I'll make sure and check on her often."

"Me, too," Nina said, thankful that she'd partnered up with a good man. A man who was back in the driver's seat, while she sat here wondering how her heart would ever recover after he left.

Shoving that from her mind, Nina got out of the vehicle, and together they went into the bank. One of the officers took them to the vault where the safety deposit boxes were stored.

The key worked right away and soon they had the box open.

"An envelope," Nina said, picking up the package with gloved hands. "Something's in here."

She opened the taped seal that held the padded yellow envelope together, while Thomas took pictures to verify. Then she pulled out a burner phone and another envelope. This one was white and sealed with heavy tape.

And it had a name written across it.

Kelly Denton. The girl who'd been shot. Nina managed to peel away the tape so they could quickly scan the letter. It told the whole tale. The senator's son had assaulted Kelly, and the two other girls had heard him bragging about it. That had started a chain of events that resulted in a cover-up and now, murder.

"We'd better take this to the police station," Thomas said. "Russo isn't going to talk, because he doesn't know what we know yet. This will hopefully give us enough information to make him tell the truth."

"I hope so. That man is creepy," Nina replied, remembering his craggy face and almost suave demeanor. "I hope he tells us who hired him, although I'm pretty sure I know who that was."

She put the phone and small envelope back into the bigger one and pressed the seal together, the bank officer her witness.

Thomas followed her out of the room and then the bank officer who'd been standing nearby guided them out the door, probably relieved that they'd been discreet, since they were investigating a possible crime.

Once they were back in the SUV, Thomas turned to her. "So you've got people watching the senator's hunting lodge."

"Yes. If he makes a move, we'll find a way to detain him. And…we're still looking for his missing son. He's probably holed up with his father." She shrugged and tugged at her seat belt. "I'm thinking one or both of them must own a shotgun. Because the shotgun attacks were far from professional grade."

"Agreed. It's all beginning to add up," Thomas said. "Let's get this evidence entered and filed, and then we'll head back to Billings. Maybe there, we can finally pin down the senator and his elusive son."

Late that night, they rolled into the Wild Iris Inn's parking lot. Surprised to find Penny and Zeke still up and sitting in the cozy parlor, Nina sent them a weary smile.

"We thought you might need a snack," Penny said, glancing over at Zeke.

"And an update," he added. "Max gave us the lowdown. Sad situation, but hopefully it'll be over soon."

After taking care of Sam, Nina returned to the dining room, where Penny had set out cheese and crackers, along with brownies and coffee.

"You'll have to teach me to cook," Nina said, fatigue tugging at her.

"I'm still learning myself," Penny admitted. "We have a very good cook who leaves things for me to present to our guests."

As they ate, Nina turned to Zeke. "Russo is willing to take a plea bargain. In fact, he's begging for one."

"I would imagine so," Zeke replied. "No movement from the lodge. It's well hidden, so that explains why not many people even knew it was there."

"But you believe the senator is hiding out there?" Thomas asked, his hand tight on his coffee cup.

"And maybe the son, too."

Nina nibbled on an oatmeal cookie. "No one connected with the Senator would tell us where the senator was, but we got the impression they knew."

"They either have no idea or they know to keep quiet," Thomas said.

"And Kelly Denton?" Nina asked, worried for

the girl's safety even though Russo was out of the picture.

"Safe," Zeke said. "We moved her to another location, just in case. If the son's around, he'll come after her. Probably with a shotgun."

"Why did they send Russo after us if they know Kelly's here?" Nina asked, shaking her head.

"You saw him up close," Thomas replied, his eyes going soft as he looked at her. "And me, well, he knows I'm here to take him, one way or another. I'm thinking Senator Slaton has been trying to cover for his son's misdeeds, and he got angry when Russo botched killing Kelly Denton and put us on his trail. He's obviously been protecting Allen all this time. Killing off the girls was an attempt to end it for good."

"So the senator and his son decided to take matters into their own hands by trying to scare us off the trail. Tried to get to Kelly Denton and then sent Russo to take care of us."

"Yeah, something like that," Thomas replied. "They sent an amateur to the hospital and then sent Russo to take care of us when the attempts to scare us didn't work."

Nina shook her head. "Kelly was so scared she wouldn't tell us anything. She's been traumatized into silence. This happens to young girls a lot. Some never tell anyone at all. When she and the other girls started receiving threats, I think she just shut down."

Zeke nodded. "We kcpt so much protection on that girl, they didn't stand a chance. I'm glad for that."

Nina nodded, careful to keep her voice low. But Penny, used to the secrecy of their work, had gone upstairs to check on her two-year-old son, Kevin. "So did Max brief the team on the contents of the box—the letter that Mya had hidden, along with the phone?"

Zeke gave her a grim glance. "Yes. But give me the details again."

Thomas sat down, a brownie in his hand. "In a nutshell, Allen Slaton drugged a girl, attacked her and then bragged about it to his friends."

"Allen Slaton assaulted Kelly Denton at the Christmas party."

"And the victim was so afraid, she held the truth inside." Nina's stomach recoiled again. "He bragged to his buddies, but he didn't realize Mya Gregory had her phone set on Record, to capture something else going on at the party. When she and her friend Kristen Banks checked their video to post it, they heard Allen Slaton's voice in the background and realized what he'd done. They found Kelly later and helped her get back to her apartment. Then they told her they knew the truth."

Zeke's frown said it all. "I guess that bond helped Kelly to cope even if she was afraid to come forward."

Nina nodded. "One of the boys saw them leaving together and got concerned. Allen Slaton asked him to watch them and track their moves. That's when he realized they probably knew."

Nina took a sip of water. "The girls came up with a plan to move the phone around, hiding it here and there. After they received some cryptic threats, Kelly Denton wrote a letter but kept it hidden, explaining what had happened to her at the party. Allen Slaton had put drugs in her drink and taken advantage of her. But she thought she'd never be able to prove it, and she was terrified, so she tried to let it go. Once the boys who were with Slaton heard there was a recording of him describing the whole thing, the three girls started receiving threats, and feared for their lives. So they did what they could to put the truth together with the evidence, only they kept it hidden, thinking they'd use it when the time was right. But one of the girls got tired of the threats and took it to another level. She started blackmailing Allen Slaton."

"The Gregory girl," Zeke said, his tone grim. "She made it worse."

"Her mom was dying of cancer. They needed the money," Nina replied. "Mrs. Gregory obviously doesn't know the truth. She thought Mya worked extra jobs to help her. We aren't going to tell her unless we have to. Knowing her daughter did this to try and save her will only make it worse for her. She'll blame herself."

"It's all there in Kelly's letter," Thomas said. "She refused to tell us the truth, because she was so scared. They threatened to kill her parents. Now she's agreed to testify. But only when she knows the senator and his son are in custody and no threat to her and her family."

"Which we hope will be soon," Zeke said, getting up. "We've got people ready to go. But you two need to rest."

Nina and Thomas both stood.

"We're rested," she said. "And now we're ready."

Thomas gave Zeke an unapologetic grin. "You heard the agent."

Nina's emotions took a tumble deep inside her heart. He'd backed her up. Thomas knew she wanted in on this and he hadn't tried to stop her. She loved him—for that and oh, so many more reasons.

When she looked up and met his gaze, she saw so much in his golden-brown eyes. Would he leave after this? Would she ever see him again? Thomas gave her that slight grin and a quick wink.

Zeke's astute gaze moved from her to Thomas and back, but he didn't seem surprised. "Okay, then. Get into your gear and load up. It's gonna be a long night."

Thomas's gut burned with a new sensation. Something had passed between Nina and him back there. Something important.

He loved her.

Crazy, since they'd met under the worst of circumstances and had been thrown together to find the truth about a grim, tragic investigation. But no wonder he loved the woman. She was stubborn and spunky and…a really good FBI agent.

As they traipsed through the woods now, feet falling on soft snow with a hardly a sound, he wanted to protect her even more. But Thomas had to let Nina do her job. He'd have her back and she'd do the same for him.

That was the thing that had connected them.

Could they make this work after the fallout from this strange case had settled down?

He sure prayed so. He prayed for a lot of things as the FBI K-9 agents spread out around the perimeter of the Slaton lodge, careful to stay in the shadows. Those girls didn't deserve this and their parents had suffered in the worst kind of way. Thomas prayed for the peace beyond understanding for Mya's dying mother and Kristen's bitter, grieving father. Kelly had a second chance and he prayed for her to get past this, too. Fear and grief had held her captive, but now she could seek the help she needed.

Glancing over at Nina, Thomas took in her tactical gear and the way her shoulders rose in a rigid, down-to-business mode.

And he prayed they could work on their kisses a little bit more after this was all over.

He saw Nina check Sam. The big dog stood at the ready, wearing protective gear, too. Then his earbud crackled to life and he stood at attention, suited in his bulletproof vest and carrying a high-powered rifle.

"Let's get on with this," she said through her mic, giving him one last glance. "I'm ready for something good to happen."

"I hear that," Thomas said, and they moved in on the lodge.

Tim Ramsey and his German shepherd partner, Frodo, approached on the right. "We have movement in the front of the structure. Looks like a big den or great room."

"Have we identified the subjects?" Thomas asked through the radio.

Max spoke up from his command post a few yards into the woods. "Positive on both senator and son. We're moving in."

They spread out, two by two. Nina and Thomas took the front door. Two locals used a battering ram to get them in.

After that, everything became a blur of voices shouting, dogs barking and the whole house lighting up inside and out as they did a sweep of both levels.

Nina rushed ahead of Thomas, her gun drawn and Sam moving up front. They could hear an agent coming from another part of the house, telling the senator to get down on the floor.

Nina made it through the front door, just before someone rushed at her from a hallway and knocked her off her feet. Allen Slaton.

Sam started barking. Nina shouted, "Hands up. Down on the floor."

The younger Slaton did as she ordered, defiance mixed with fright in his pretty-boy features.

Nina called to Sam, "Guard!"

Sam stood between the boy and the door, the rottweiler growling. The kid looked terrified, his eyes wide, his hair on end. "Dad?" he called. "Dad? I can't get away."

He tried to stand.

Thomas stood behind Nina, his boots hitting on the wooden entryway, his weapon raised. "Stop right there, son. Hands up. Don't do anything stupid."

Allen Slaton started to cry, and sank to his knees. "Dad?"

Sam growled again and held his position, his snout aimed at the boy, who was now kneeling with his hands in the air.

Nina stepped between the dog and the young man. "It's over." Then she shot a relieved glance at Thomas and read the boy his rights, while the other agents brought the senator into the den just off the front hallway and sat him on a chair.

Nina commanded Sam to stay and then turned to Allen Slaton. Thomas watched as she went to pat him down.

The boy raised his arms, but quickly went for something in his back pocket, his expression full of rage and fear, his eyes on Nina. Thomas saw the weapon and didn't think twice.

"Nina, look out," he shouted. And then, after making sure she was safe, he shot Allen Slaton.

ELEVEN

"You did it again." Ignoring all the action around them, Nina stared up at Thomas, her heart beginning to slow down, her pulse less jumpy now.

"Yep. Just can't seem to stop myself from protecting you." He grinned, but she saw the darkness in his eyes, along with something else that made her want to hold him tight. "I'm sorry the boy is dead, but I had no choice. He could have killed you."

"But he didn't. I had my weapon and I had Sam." Instead of fussing at Thomas, she leaned up and gave him a quick peck on the jaw. "And now I have you."

She turned to get back into the fray, but his hand on her arm stopped her. "Are you sure about that? I mean, I don't back down."

"Neither do I, cowboy. As soon as we tie up these loose ends, we're going home for Christmas."

Thomas watched her walk away, that tough-girl stride colliding with the softness of her gentle kiss.

"We're gonna need your statement and…well, you know the drill," Max West said without preamble from behind Thomas.

"Understood," he answered, turning to find the man's eyes wide with realization. Thomas wondered if Max had witnessed that quick breach of protocol. "I'll call my people and explain. I know the routine. I hate this part of the job, though. I killed that young man."

"Yes, because he had a weapon and he pulled it out after both Nina and you warned him." Max looked to the patrol car where a shocked and dazed Senator Richard Slaton sat with hand-cuffs on his wrists. "The irony is that they hired a known assassin to kill three innocent girls—all to protect their good name and the status quo. In his desire to shield his son, the senator broke the law and tried to cover it all up. Now his only son is dead, and the senator will probably be in prison for a long, long time.

"Russo's talking now and Slaton is beyond caring about his precious image anymore," Max finished. "We've got reports to file and then we can close this one out." Rubbing the back of his neck, he added, "I've got to move on to these possible-arson fires. Tim's taking the lead on that one, thankfully. His K-9 partner's expertise is in sniffing out accelerants."

"Tim's a good agent. But then, your whole team seems solid." Thomas hesitated and then said, "If you're done with us, Nina and I want to go talk to Kelly Denton and let her know she's safe."

"Okay," Max said, turning to get back to work. Then he pivoted and gave Thomas a hard stare. "Don't take her away from us, Deputy Marshal."

Thomas pondered that for a moment. "You mean Agent Atkins? Hadn't planned on it. I've always had a hankering to live in Montana. Now seems like a good time to act on that notion."

Max cracked a quick, fleeting grin. "Does Agent Atkins know that yet?"

"No, not yet, but I aim to fill her in real soon."

A couple hours later, dawn started a gentle approach over the mountains, coloring the snow-tipped peaks in a shimmering pink-gold light.

Thomas stood with Nina at the door of her room at the inn. He wanted to hold her and kiss her and tell her he'd never leave her. But that would scare her away...

They'd gone to tell Kelly Denton and her parents that Allen Slaton was dead and that both Russo and the senator were in jail. Even if the senator got out on bail, Kelly would be safe. The FBI and US Marshal Department would make sure of that.

Right now, he was concerned about Nina. She took helping people to heart.

"If you ask me again if I'm okay, I might deck you," she said, reading his mind with all the precision of a high-powered flashlight.

"*Are* you okay?" he asked anyway.

She fisted her hand and knocked on his biceps twice. "I guess that didn't really hurt you at all, did it?"

"Told you I'm tough," he said, gathering her into his arms. "I've died a thousand deaths since I met you, but I sure like being around you."

Nina knew that feeling. Wanting to protect him and take care of him and never let him go out there again. But then, he was big and brawny and... beautiful. Why did love hurt and heal all at the same time?

"Think you can handle me, cowboy?"

He tugged her close and grinned down at her. "Yes, ma'am. I'll give it my best shot."

"Then kiss me like you mean it," she quipped.

He did, and then he followed her inside and held her close on the love seat by the fire. "Let's watch the sunrise coming over the mountaintop," he said. "Then I'll let you get some sleep."

Nina stirred and sat straight up, remembering where she was and why she wasn't at her little house anymore. She'd have to get that fixed soon. Then she smelled fresh coffee and bacon. A knock at her door made her hurry and freshen up while Sam's ears perked up.

"Come in," she called, stepping out of the tiny bathroom, her warm robe cocooning her.

She was having a good dream.

And in it, a tall Texan was standing at the door with breakfast and a red rose on a tray.

"Can I keep you?" she asked in a husky squeak of delight.

Thomas smiled at her. "I don't come cheap. I like a lot of groceries. Even Penny's complaining about that."

"I think I can manage buying more food," Nina said, getting up and wishing she'd brought pretty clothes to the inn with her.

Then she glanced around. Sam sat watching them probably amazed at the sizzle of something more than bacon moving through the small space. "Ah, Thomas, where did you sleep? Not out in front of my door, I hope."

"I went to my room and was out like a light," he said, while he arranged the tray on the bistro table by the bay window. Then he petted the rottweiler on the head. "But Sam told me I really missed out on a lot. Said you snore. Told me it's the cutest thing, so delicate and—"

A throw pillow hit him upside his head. Dodging it, he said, "Hey, don't mess up this wonderful breakfast Penny and I prepared for you."

"I don't snore." Nina marched toward him and glanced at the clock. "It's late. I should get to work."

"Max said your vacation officially starts today, remember?"

She let out a little breath. "I'd forgotten I have five days off. And it's two days until Christmas. No wonder my mom's been calling."

"You might want to let her know you're safe and sound and you'll be home for Christmas," Thomas said as he set out plates full of eggs, bacon and toast. With some fruit on the side. Then he held out the rose with a flourish.

The man was full of surprises.

Nina took a sniff and let the sweet scent surround her, then sank into a chair and tried to drain her coffee. Putting down the dainty Christmas cup, she said, "Uh, Thomas…"

He stood across from her and stared down at her. "Yes, I'd love to go home with you for Christmas and meet your family. And no, you can't back out of it now because I'm pretty sure one day in the future, they will become my family, too."

Was he proposing to her?

Did she want him to propose to her?

"You're kind of confident," she said, hoping she didn't look as confused as she felt, and wishing she could be as confident as him. She'd never been impulsive, but now she wanted to dive right into breakfast and into being with Thomas.

He sat down and grabbed a piece of toast. He looked fresh and alive, and he smelled like the pines in high country. He wore a button-up shirt and jeans.

Off duty but on the prowl.

She liked him. Loved him. "Are you sure about all of this?"

How was she going to survive having him around her judgmental, outspoken family?

He leaned back and chewed on his toast, his eyes moving over her in a catlike fashion. "I'm pretty sure that I want to spend some time with you, no guns and no regrets."

"I have to figure out things, Thomas."

"About me? About us?"

"Yes, and about my house. It's a mess. I need to go by there and probably meet with the landlord and the insurance people." She stared at her bacon. "This is happening so fast."

"Eat your breakfast," he said, as calm as a sleeping lion. "Call your mom. Your landlord is aware of what happened to your house. He promises to have someone out to look at it today. You can figure out the insurance stuff and get with your landlord and then grab what you need to go home for Christmas."

"You talked to my landlord?"

"Max had Dylan talk to him, since you were kind of busy."

"Five or six days busy," she said. "We've only known each other a week. Isn't that kind of strange?"

Thomas stopped eating and stood up. "Okay, if you're not comfortable with me going with you, I'll understand. It won't be the first time I've spent Christmas alone."

Nina's stomach roiled. She'd invited him. She

didn't want him to be alone during the holidays. Was he walking out on her? Well, she had told him she wasn't sure.

Feeling like the worst kind of tease, she said, "Thomas?"

"Nina, if you're not ready for this, we can try again once things settle down. I get it. We've been through a lot this past week and you need some time to debrief. Then, of course, I'm a lot to deal with. I have a dangerous job and I travel at the drop of hat. It works for me, but it's never worked in a relationship." Putting a hand on the doorjamb, he added, "Or at least, it hasn't before."

Then he was gone, moving fast for such a big man.

She waited a beat or two and then glanced over at Sam.

The dog looked at the door, woofed, and then set his doleful eyes on her. *"Go after him."*

Nina's heart took over her common sense. Grabbing suede booties to protect her bare feet from the snow, she stumbled down the stairs, still tugging one on.

Thomas was headed for the front door.

She rushed toward it and slammed it shut, then turned to see his surprised expression. "You big oaf, I want you to...be my date for Christmas. I'm scared and stupid, and I thought you'd be like my brothers and dad, but you're not. You accept me, Thomas. You get me. We both have the kind of careers that scare normal people, so I'm okay with you having to leave." Grabbing him by the collar, she added, "But don't you ever walk away from me again."

He let out a breath, his gaze softening with relief. "I had to be sure."

She yanked him into her arms and kissed him. "Did that make you sure?"

"I don't know. Maybe a few more times."

Kissing him again, she breathed a thankful prayer.

"Will it always be like this?" she asked.

"Probably worse." He kissed her back. "And better."

"Okay, I can live with that," she said. "Let me get changed and we'll get going. We've got lots to do today."

Christmas Day

Nina showed Thomas the turn to the winding road up the mountain. Her entire family was waiting for them.

"They'll try to pick you apart," she warned, her tone shaky. "We could go somewhere else for Christmas."

"You're not getting cold feet, are you?" he asked, still amazed that she'd taken a leap of faith. "I mean, we brought gifts and I've got on my game face."

"No, I want you to be here. I want to be here with you. But you've heard how my brothers are. They'll test you to the limit."

"Bring it."

"My dad will do a background check on you."

"I don't mind that a bit."

"My mom will ask you fifty questions."

"I'll give her fifty answers."

The big cabin was a solid, rambling, worn, towering structure that looked as if it had been carved into the mountainside. Snow-covered and decorated with pine wreaths draped in bright red bows, it looked like the perfect Christmas card.

"They'll all be staring out the window," she said as the two of them got out of the truck.

Thomas met her by her door and whispered, "Then let's give them something to talk about."

He kissed her and then turned to face the house. "Nina, in spite of the horror that brought us together, I'm thanking God right now. This is the best Christmas I've ever had."

Sam danced around while they kissed again. Then the big dog woofed and stared up at them. *It's about time.*

Before they could part, the front door opened and one tiny woman and five domineering men rushed out to greet them.

Thomas grinned and shook hands and felt as if his heart had been rearranged and tied up with one of those bright red bows.

"Welcome home," Nina's mom said, hugging her daughter tight. But she was looking at Thomas.

* * * * *

If you enjoyed CLASSIFIED K-9 UNIT CHRISTMAS, look for the other books in the CLASSIFIED K-9 UNIT series:

GUARDIAN by Terri Reed
SHERIFF by Laura Scott
SPECIAL AGENT by Valerie Hansen
BOUNTY HUNTER by Lynette Eason
BODYGUARD by Shirlee McCoy
TRACKER by Lenora Worth

Dear Reader,

While this subject matter was disturbing, I enjoyed working with the talented Terri Reed in this two-in-one story. It was exciting to put a strong female FBI agent with an equally strong US Deputy Marshal. Nina and Thomas stole my heart. I knew their story would be a challenge since they both wanted the same thing—to get the bad guy. And yet, they needed each other, too.

Sometimes in trying to be strong, we forget that God sees our weaknesses and helps us overcome them. Having faith gives us strength beyond measure. But accepting God's help can be hard to do at times.

I hope you have a good Christmas. Think of Nina taking Thomas home to a place of love and happiness. I want you to feel that, too, no matter where you are in life.

Until next time, may the angels watch over you. Always.

Lenora Worth

YULETIDE STALKING

Terri Reed

Have I not commanded you? Be strong and courageous.
Do not be afraid; do not be discouraged, for the Lord
your God will be with you wherever you go.
–*Joshua* 1:9

ONE

The cold December night air smelled of burned rubber and the lingering acrid odor of consuming flames. If not for the quick response of the Billings, Montana, fire department, the downtown tire store would have been a total loss.

Agent Tim Ramsey, a junior member of the FBI Tactical K-9 Unit headquartered in Billings, sat back on his haunches next to his canine partner. The three-year-old German shepherd, named Frodo, specialized in accelerant detection. They both had on booties to protect the scene and themselves.

This was the third fire in as many weeks. The first two were residential properties on the outskirts of town. A knot of frustration formed in Tim's chest. With Christmas just a few days away, the last thing anyone needed was a firebug on the loose.

Frodo kept his intense gaze on the floor, using his primary alert of sitting at attention. This was the dog's way of letting Tim know he smelled something of interest in the ash-covered area at the back corner of the store. It was the same area the firefighters suspected was the point of origin. Frodo and Tim's job was to root out the cause.

Tim trusted Frodo's keen sense of smell with his life. The dog's ability to detect odors and differentiate them with accuracy was what made Frodo and other canines so valuable in law enforcement.

With gloved hands, Tim gently sifted through the rubble, looking for clues. He lifted a piece of burned rubber. His stomach sank. Beneath lay the remnants of what he suspected was the cause of the fire. He knew what the forensic team would find upon analysis of the debris: cigarette ash, fibers from pillow stuffing and fragments of a generic matchbook. And trace elements of gasoline, just like in the other two fires. All indicators of arson.

Tim tagged the evidence with yellow markers, rose and addressed the Billings fire chief. "Sir, I believe our serial arsonist has struck again."

He could only hope and pray they caught the fiend before more fires were set, or the holiday season would go up in smoke and lives could be in jeopardy.

Christmas music drifted into the kitchen of the Billings Homeless Shelter. Trying to relax and enjoy this special time of year, Vickie Petrov hummed along to the upbeat tune as she rolled out more dough for her family's famous biscuits.

As was their tradition, she and her parents were serving the homeless on Christmas Eve. Because they owned a bakery, they made biscuits and pies, while other eateries in town provided turkeys and all the side dishes for the meal.

Vickie preferred to stay behind the scenes, where no one paid any attention to her. Wiping her brow with the sleeve of her thermal shirt, she glanced out the small window above the sink. Fat snowflakes fell from the sky. An involuntary tremor of dread worked over her limbs. Another white Christmas.

Having grown up in Billings, she was accustomed to the cold winters. Though she enjoyed bundling up, hiding beneath layers of sweaters, scarves and big jackets that kept her warm and safe, she preferred the bluebell sky of summer, where there were no nightmares lurking in the shadows.

Winter always brought back memories of... things she'd rather forget.

Another shiver chased over her skin. She shoved it away. She was safe here. No need to let the past intrude on such a festive night. Still, she couldn't shake the strange sense of dread that had camped out in her chest for months now. There was no reason to believe she was being watched or followed, yet everywhere she went, the small hairs at the base of her neck would quiver with fear.

More than once, she thought she'd glimpsed Ken's face in the crowd. But then she'd look again and he wouldn't be there. It was just her imagination run amok. Ken was most likely in California, living the dream he professed to deserve.

Forcing him and the simmering anger clogged with fear from her mind, she used the round cutter mold and cut out two dozen biscuits, then set them on a baking sheet and popped them in the oven.

The double doors of the kitchen swung open and her mother strode through, with two plastic bags of garbage in tow.

Affection filled Vickie. "Here, Mom, let me take care of that."

Irena Petrov relinquished her hold on the bags. Beneath her white baker's apron, she wore a sweater with a Christmas motif of reindeer romping in a meadow, strands of colored lights adorning their antlers. Her silver hair was twisted into a fancy bun at the nape of her neck.

Her clear blue-gray eyes danced with joy. "I wish you'd come out and join the festivities. Your father and Pastor John are setting up a karaoke machine so they can sing Christmas carols."

Vickie laughed. "I'll come watch when the singing starts."

"Okay, then." Irena checked on the pies. "These look wonderful, Vic. You do us proud with your baking." A shadow crossed her mother's face. "I wish you'd reconsider going back to college to get your business degree. I want you to be fully ready to take over the bakery one day."

Vickie forced herself not to flinch at the reminder of her broken dreams of graduating from the prestigious college that had granted her a scholarship. "I will be ready, Mom. The online courses I'm taking will prepare me just fine."

"You're alone too much," Irena chided gently. "It's been three years since you came home. Don't you think it's time to try again? You'll never find a nice young man to marry working behind the counter at the bakery."

"You never know, Mom," Vickie teased. "Daddy was behind the counter in his family's bakery when you met him."

Irena's face softened with love. "True. But that was in the old country." Her parents had immigrated to America from the Ukraine shortly after they married. "The world has changed so much since then. Why don't you try one of those online dating sites?"

Vickie sighed. "Mom, I'm not ready to date."

She feared she'd never be. Of course, her mom and dad didn't know the whole truth. She'd wanted to protect them from the depth of her pain. After the assault by her date, Ken, during her third year at the prestigious college in Boston, she doubted she'd ever be ready to let a man close again.

Yanking open the back door, she stepped outside with the two bags of garbage. Caution whispered across her flesh, raising goose bumps everywhere. She glanced around. She was alone. Safe.

Refusing to give in to the old fear, she set the

bags on the ground so she could use both hands to lift the heavy lid of the Dumpster. Her skin prickled from the frigid temperature. The cold metal against her palms nearly made her lose her grip.

The smell of burning cigarettes close by mingled with the stench of trash. Vickie wrinkled her nose, feeling the hairs at the back of her neck rising in alarm. Unease twisted in her stomach. Anxious to get back inside, she quickly hefted the two bags into the container and then let the lid fall back in place with a noisy clank.

Before she could return to the safety of the kitchen, two strong bands of steel wrapped around her middle, trapping her forearms at her sides. Terror jolted through her brain like electricity. Her heart slammed into her ribs.

A scream built in her chest.

Her brain fought through the stunned panic. She'd taken self-defense classes at the local community center, determined to never again let anyone hurt her.

She bent her elbows, cupped her left hand over her right fist and used her right elbow as a battering ram into her attacker's rib cage as she twisted to face him where she'd be able to use her knees, feet and hands to strike out, to disable him.

Her assailant grunted, released her and bolted, running away into the dark.

Thrown off balance, Vickie stumbled, catching herself so she didn't take a header into the snow.

She covered her heart with a hand and sent up a prayer of gratitude for her safety even as her mind grappled with what had just happened. Who was the man? Why had he grabbed her?

For a fleeting moment, an image of Ken's face reared up in her mind. That wasn't possible. She was mixing up the past with the present.

Trembling, she hurried toward the shelter's back door. She had to call the police. They had to catch the guy so he didn't attack someone else. She prayed the cops would believe her. The last time she'd dealt with law enforcement hadn't gone well.

A soft popping sound froze her in place with her hand on the doorknob. Fire ignited in the debris near the Dumpster. Flames shot up the side of the building, consuming the shelter's back wall in seconds.

Adrenaline spiking, she yanked open the back door and ran inside, screaming, *"Fire!"*

Tim secured a weather and bulletproof vest around Frodo's torso and attached the lead to the loop on his collar before releasing the dog from his special compartment in the black FBI-issued SUV. Keeping the dog at his side, he headed to the latest fire scene.

Cold air seeped beneath the collar of his thick black jacket emblazoned with the FBI Tactical K-9 Unit on the breast pocket. He was thankful he'd pulled on a black knit beanie to protect his head and ears from the icy temperature.

With a nod at the police officers stationed around the perimeter, he and Frodo walked past the barriers keeping the horde of people congregating on the sidewalk out of the firefighters' way and headed into the action. Heat emanated from the homeless shelter as the firefighters worked to put out the inferno.

Assessing the situation, he noted the amount of damage to the back side of the building. The flames had traveled up to the second floor. Black smoked curled into the night sky.

Fire Chief Ed Clark waved Tim over to where he stood. "I'm glad you're here. The fire burned hot and fast. We got to the blaze quickly. It seems our arsonist has struck again. We have a witness," Chief Clark stated and walked toward a group of civilians huddled together apart from the rest of the crowd.

Tim and Frodo followed the chief. If the witness could identify the firebug, that would be an appreciated Christmas gift, indeed.

"Miss Petrov," Chief Clark said. "This is Agent Ramsey from the FBI. He and his partner help with our fire investigations. Can you please tell him what you told me?"

Tim halted beside the chief, and Frodo sat at his side. Surprise washed over Tim. He recognized

Irena and Sasha Petrov. The Petrov Bakery was a favorite with the FBI Tactical K-9 Unit.

Then his gaze landed on the pretty ash-blond woman sandwiched between her parents. Tim had tried on several occasions to engage in conversation with her, but she hadn't reciprocated the effort.

Not that he was interested in pursuing anything. He was a confirmed bachelor. He'd learned the painful lesson of what happened when he let his heart get attached. Giving away a part of himself only to have it flung back in his face wasn't something he ever intended to repeat.

"Mr. and Mrs. Petrov." He smiled encouragingly at Vickie, hoping to assuage her usual skittishness. She stared at him with big blue eyes from beneath the brim of her snow parka's hood. "Miss Petrov. You all were here at the shelter tonight?"

"Yes, we help feed the homeless on Christmas," Sasha explained. He was a tall, slender man with a graying goatee and silver hair slicked back from his high forehead. "It's tradition."

"A nice one." The church Tim went to collected coats for the homeless. He'd donated several new ones. Every act of kindness helped those in need.

"Go on, Vic," Irena urged. She was several inches shorter than her husband and her daughter. She wore a red wool coat with a matching felt hat covering her head. "Tell the agent what happened."

Vickie lifted her chin as if steeling herself to

talk to him. There was apprehension in her gaze. "I was taking out the garbage when I smelled cigarette smoke."

"Did you smell gasoline, too?" Anticipation revved in Tim's veins. "So you saw the person?"

She frowned. "No gasoline. It all happened so fast. I only caught a glimpse of his face in the shadows."

"Maybe with the help of a forensic artist, you'd be able to describe him enough for us to get an ID." This could be the break in the case they needed.

"I could try." Her tone suggested she doubted her success.

Tim had seen the FBI forensic artist work wonders with witnesses who were convinced they had nothing to offer. "You saw the guy start the fire?"

He glanced at the shelter. The flames had rapidly crawled up the building. Not the same modus operandi as the previous fires. But he wouldn't know for sure until the fire chief gave him the all clear to work the scene, which might not be until tomorrow.

"No. I only heard it after…"

Tim focused back on her. "After?"

"Maybe he dropped the cigarette when he grabbed me."

Her softly spoken words clanged through Tim's brain like a fire alarm. "He grabbed you? Why didn't you lead with that?" This took things to a whole new level.

Irena gasped. "You didn't tell us. Are you okay?"

Sasha put a protective arm around his daughter. "Did he hurt you?"

"I'm fine." Vickie leaned into her father. "I jabbed him with my elbow and he ran off."

"Impressive." Tim was relieved she was unharmed. "Good for you. Not many people would keep their head enough to react appropriately. Did the man say anything?"

"No, nothing. Like I said, he ran off. The fire started seconds later."

"She came inside yelling there was a fire, and got everyone out safely," Irena said, pride lacing her words.

Tim met Vickie's gaze. Respect for her grew tenfold. "You're a hero."

Her chin dipped in a shy way that Tim found endearing. "No. I did what anyone would have done."

"All the same, you saved lives tonight," Tim said. He admired how genuinely self-effacing she was, not at all trying to gain the limelight for acting quickly.

She gave him a soft smile. He could tell she was pleased by his words and for some odd reason that made him happy.

"Sir! You must stay back," A patrol officer restrained a tall man with a bald head who was trying to push his way past the barrier.

Vickie sucked in a breath and shrank back, practically hiding behind her parents.

Tim's heart rate picked up. "Is that the man who attacked you?"

Could this be the firebug?

TWO

"No." Vickie slipped out from behind her parents, embarrassed by her reflex to hide from the man pointing toward her. "That's Greg Sherman, the neighborhood day security guard." She couldn't let Tim think Greg was the man who'd attacked her. She paused.

A chill chased down her spine.

He wasn't, was he?

She'd have recognized him, right?

She had to admit Greg and her assailant were both tall and bulky. But that could describe so many men. Besides, Greg wouldn't hurt her.

But she'd thought the same of Ken once upon a time. She'd been wrong. Was she wrong now?

Fear tightened a noose around her throat.

She glanced at Greg. He waved. She automatically raised her hand in response before she thought better of encouraging him. Her fingers curled into a fist.

Tim leveled a pointed look at her. "He's a friend of yours?"

More like an irritant. A harmless one, or so she'd thought until now. Her shoulder muscles tightened. "Our relationship is complicated. I've known him forever."

"If Greg works days, what's he doing here tonight?" Tim asked. Without waiting for an answer, he turned and, with his dog at his side, strode toward the barricade line.

From over her mother's head, Vickie watched Tim stop to address Greg and keep him from forcing his way past the cordoned-off zone. She should have guessed he would show up. He always appeared out of the blue when she least expected him. Most likely he was the cause of the unsettled feeling she'd had lately.

She really wished he'd take the hint and go away. She'd turned down every one of his many invitations to dinner, the movies and other outings since she returned from college three years ago. Had he finally realized she wasn't interested and attacked her for it? Her pulse sped up.

But why now? And why would he want to hurt the shelter?

After a few moments of intense conversation, Tim and his partner walked away, leaving Greg behind the barricade. What had they talked about?

Her?

She blew out a breath of frustration and watched Tim talk to the Billings police chief, no doubt telling him about the attack. Would Chief Fielding take her seriously? She pressed her lips together.

Jamming her hands into her pockets to keep from fidgeting, she struggled to calm herself. Her nerves were strung out from all the attention focused on her. It had taken every ounce of self-possession not to squirm under Tim's regard while he'd questioned her. And his words of praise had made her heart bump against her breastbone in a funny way.

Just as it did every time he came into the bakery. He always started up a conversation, usually about the weather or about the different pastries. She knew he liked his coffee with almond milk creamer and had a preference for apricot filling. He seemed like a nice guy. Kind and considerate. But then again, what did she know?

She'd thought the same thing of Ken. He'd been an intern with one of the college's leading researchers, on track to graduate magna cum laude when they'd met in the library. He'd been charming and attentive and she'd been so flattered when he asked her out.

Three dates later, he tried to force himself on her. If not for the grace of God and her roommate's timely arrival, he'd have finished what he'd started.

Afterward, he'd taunted her, calling her a tease for not giving him what he wanted. What he deserved. He'd turned into someone else and made her question herself. How had she not seen him for who he really was? Had she been blinded by his suave demeanor and gentlemanly ways?

When she'd reported him to campus police, they blew her off, believing his lies that she was trying to ruin his reputation because he'd refused her advances. As if she were the one in the wrong.

She'd even shown the dean and the officer the bruises left by Ken's hands, but the marks hadn't swayed either man whom she'd thought were there to protect her. Instead, they'd dismissed the bruises, saying the dark spots could have been from anything and didn't prove Ken had assaulted her. She wasn't sure what pull Ken had with the school, but whatever it was, it was enough to keep him from trouble.

She'd found out the hard way that she'd made a mistake in trusting those in authority. A mistake she wouldn't make again.

Even with a handsome FBI agent.

Tim and the police chief were now talking with Lacey Klems, who ran the shelter, and Pastor John, both of whom were clearly upset. Vickie's heart went out to the dozens of people who had nowhere else to stay on this frosty Christmas Eve.

There had to be a way to find the displaced individuals warm accommodations for the foreseeable future, until the shelter could be repaired.

Another commotion from the opposite direction drew her attention.

"I demand to be let through. Who's in charge here?" A short, rotund man in a trench coat that touched the toes of his black wing tipped shoes, and a fur hat, gestured widely toward the building. His voice carried as he shouted at the police officer keeping him out of the cordoned-off area.

Vickie pulled a face. "What is Mr. Johnson doing here?"

"I believe he owns this building," her dad replied.

As well as the one they rented for the bakery. Vickie wasn't a fan of their landlord.

Pastor John and Lacey Klems hurried to the blockade.

Vickie's father sighed. "I should go help Pastor and Ms. Klems. Mr. Johnson can be a bear to deal with. He's been unreasonable since summer. I'm not sure what has him so prickly."

"We'll both go." Vickie's mom tucked her arm around her husband's. The two marched over to show support to their pastor and friend.

Feeling vulnerable and conspicuous standing by herself, Vickie hurried to catch up. Pride for her parents filled her chest. They were good, steady people with hearts of gold. And they were still very much in love even after thirty-plus years of marriage. She wanted a relationship such as theirs, but doubted she'd ever find someone to whom she could risk giving her heart.

As she stepped next to her parents, she heard Mr. Johnson say, "I knew this wasn't a good idea."

Lacey fiddled with the wool scarf around her neck. "Barry, please, you know as well as I do how much the city needs the shelter."

"So you keep telling me," Mr. Johnson huffed.

"Serving so many meals in one night. Did the oven explode? Did someone leave the gas stove on?"

"No, sir." Vickie's dad stepped up. "We don't know what exactly happened."

Mr. Johnson narrowed his gaze on him. "What are you doing here?"

"We provided the biscuits and dessert for the Christmas meal." Though her father kept his voice polite, she knew that tone. It was the one he used when their supplier tried to short them on the good chocolate.

Mr. Johnson turned to address the Billings patrol officer standing nearby. "Did they cause this?"

Vickie gasped. Anger spread through her chest, overheating her beneath her parka. How dare their landlord accuse them of starting the fire! The man was a miser and a bully. She always dreaded the days he came to the bakery to collect his rent. He'd help himself to a pastry or two, uninvited, as if getting free food was his due.

The patrolman raised his eyebrows. "The fire investigation hasn't been done yet, sir."

"Barry, the fire didn't start in the kitchen," Pastor John told him. "Please, don't jump to conclusions. We—"

"You told me you could handle this," Mr. Johnson said, before he could finish speaking. "We'll have to seriously reconsider the future of the shelter once the building is repaired."

"Now, Barr—" The clergyman stopped speaking as Mr. Johnson raised a hand.

"Don't *now Barry* me," Mr. Johnson said. "I was reluctant to allow the shelter into the building to begin with and apparently I was right to be concerned." He gestured to the smoldering structure.

Knowing the loss of the shelter would be a terrible blow to the pastor, Vickie tapped into the adrenaline coursing through her veins and stepped beyond her fear of drawing attention to herself to say, "There's no way anyone could have predicted a fire."

He stared down his wide nose. "Except one happened, now, didn't it?"

"Barry, there's no need to snap at Vickie," Pastor John said.

Tim and Frodo came over. For some reason their presence gave her a measure of comfort as she scooted to the side to make room for them.

"What's the problem here?" Tim asked.

"Who are you?" Mr. Johnson countered. "Are you in charge?"

"FBI agent Tim Ramsey." He showed the man his badge. "We're investigating the fire. What is your purpose here?"

"That's my building," Mr. Johnson said. "This is going to raise my insurance rates and has ruined my Christmas celebration with my family."

Vickie couldn't believe the landlord's level of insensitivity. Surely he realized the inconvenience to his evening was not nearly as devastating as it was to those who called the shelter home for the night.

"This fire has ruined everyone's Christmas," Tim stated in a firm tone. "Without the shelter, most of these people will be struggling to find somewhere safe to get out of the cold."

Vickie wanted to applaud Tim for putting Mr. Johnson in his place and validating her thoughts. Admiration for the agent spread through her chest like frosting on cookies. She met his gaze and offered him a smile of appreciation. Something flared in his eyes, sending ribbons of warmth winding through her. The unsettling sensation knocked her back a step.

"I want to know who started this fire," Mr. Johnson demanded. "I'll have to file a claim."

Tim turned his attention back to the landlord. "Sir, you'll receive a copy of the report once it is finished."

Mr. Johnson harrumphed. "My nephew, Joseph, is a firefighter. I'm sure he'll fill me in on what I need to know."

For a moment Tim's eyes narrowed. "Until we release the scene, you will stand back behind the barricade and let us do our jobs."

Vickie fought to hide a smile. She shouldn't gloat over Tim's dressing down the arrogant Mr. Johnson, but she was relieved someone had no qualms about standing up to the bully.

Turning away from the man in dismissal, Tim addressed Vickie and her parents. "You're free to go."

"Thank you, Agent Ramsey," her dad said, and shook his hand. "We won't be leaving quite yet." He turned to Pastor John. "We can open the bakery and provide sandwiches for everyone."

Pastor John clapped her dad on the back. "You are a good man, Sasha. Let's round everyone up and head over there."

"Vickie," Tim said, stopping her from following her parents, Pastor John and Lacey Klems. "I'll come by the bakery tomorrow to arrange for you to sit with a forensic artist."

"But tomorrow is Christmas Day," she said. "Surely it can wait until the twenty-sixth."

"Crime doesn't observe the holidays," Tim said softly.

Her stomach churned. "What will happen to all the people who were counting on staying at the shelter?"

Tim's lips pressed together in a grim line. "I don't know. Police Chief Fielding will make arrangements. I'm sure he'll contact the Red Cross."

Vickie slid her gaze back to Mr. Johnson, who was now on the phone, no doubt with his insurance company. She wondered how many buildings he owned in Billings. And if there was a space for a makeshift shelter. She bit the inside of her lip. The man's altruism was a shallow well, but she had to try.

"Are you okay?" Tim asked.

She stared into his blue-green eyes. His question sparked a fire of determination in her belly. She needed to be strong, to stand up for those who couldn't. Bravery wasn't her strong suit, but tonight she needed to find her courage. "No, I'm not."

The concern darkening Tim's expression sent her pulse thundering. It was his job to be concerned, she reminded herself, and focused her attention on Mr. Johnson. As soon as he finished his call, Vickie waved to him. "Mr. Johnson, can I speak to you?"

His brow crinkled with apparent irritation. He walked to the barricade separating them. "What now?"

She could feel Tim's curious gaze on her. His presence gave her strength. Gathering her courage, she said, "Would you have a space in one of your other buildings that could be made into a temporary shelter?"

He frowned. "What do I look like? A charity?"

"It's a sound idea," Tim said. "How many buildings do you own? Are they full?"

Mr. Johnson snorted. "I'd have to check with my leasing agent to see what empty space we have and what the rent would be."

"Rent?" Vickie couldn't stomach the man's

greediness. "Really? On Christmas Eve?" She turned away from him in disgust. "Maybe the high school gym could accommodate everyone for tonight? I'll go ask Chief Fielding."

Tim put his hand on her arm, keeping her from walking away. "Mr. Johnson, get your leasing agent on the phone now."

"And ruin his Christmas, too?" The older man shook his head. "I can't help you."

Tim stepped closer, towering over the landlord, and lowered his voice. "Sir, the community would appreciate your generosity and goodwill in helping out those less fortunate. I'm sure the media would report such kindness in the face of this tragedy." He shrugged. "Or they might report your refusal to help."

Mr. Johnson's eyes widened. He pushed forward a step. "Are you threatening me?"

Frodo let out a low growl. The man jumped back.

"Not at all," Tim stated. "Just reminding you this incident tonight will make the news. In fact…" He tipped his head toward where the local news crew were filming the shelter fire and interviewing bystanders. "What kind of man do you want to be viewed as?"

Mr. Johnson's lip curled as he yanked his cell phone from his pocket. "I'll see what I can do." He turned away to talk to his leasing agent.

"Wow," Vickie said beneath her breath, so only Tim would hear. "You handled him well."

He cupped her elbow and drew her away from the crowd of people. "Sometimes people need a nudge to do the right thing."

"Sad but true."

"You'll need to prepare yourself as well," Tim told her. "The news people will want to talk to you, too."

Anxiety twisted in her gut. "I don't want to be on camera. What if the man who attacked me decides to come after me again?"

"Don't worry. I won't let anything happen to you," he told her. "I've already spoken to Police Chief Fielding and he will have a patrol officer stationed outside your house."

She'd rather have Tim and his dog for protection. She blinked in surprise at the realization. He was a law officer. The representation of everything she'd come to loathe after the attack at college. She'd turned to the authorities for help but had been brushed off as if she didn't matter.

Did she really want to rely on this man for her safety?

It was better than the alternative.

At least Tim seemed to take her seriously.

"Agent Ramsey," Mr. Johnson called out, drawing their attention.

Tim's warm hand settled on the small of Vickie's back. Surprise washed over her and she nearly lost her footing on the icy sidewalk. He steadied her and guided her toward the barricade. Her mouth went dry and her heart raced. She hadn't let anyone get this physically close in a very long time.

"Yes?" Tim said, as they drew to a halt.

Looking as if he had swallowed a lemon, Mr. Johnson said, "One of my buildings a few blocks from here has space. You can relocate the shelter on a purely temporary basis. The leasing agent will meet you there with the keys."

Delighted by the news, Vickie could have hugged the man, but instead, she smiled. "Thank you, Mr. Johnson."

His gaze flicked to her and away. "A couple of days at most. I'm a businessman, not a philanthropist."

Vickie and Tim shared a glance. *No news flash there.*

"Either way, the gesture is appreciated," she said.

Mr. Johnson made a noise in his throat and left.

"Merry Christmas," she called after him.

"I'll tell Police Chief Fielding and help him organize a crew to transition everyone over," Tim said.

"I'll go tell my parents and Pastor John," Vickie replied.

As she hurried to where they stood talking to the many displaced shelter occupants, the now familiar sensation of being watched shimmied down her spine. She glanced behind her at Tim, but he had his back to her.

Looking around, she met several curious glances from those on the other side of the barricade and from many of the firefighters, who's faces were obscured by their masks, now wrapping up their hoses and putting away their equipment. She searched each face, half afraid to find herself locking eyes with Ken. But he wasn't in the crowd. There was no way he'd be in Billings. She hadn't seen him in three years. It was her imagination. Or her fear that one day she would see him again.

There was nothing concrete to warrant the tingling chill tiptoeing over her flesh.

Yet she couldn't stop the questions bouncing around her head. Was her attacker among the gawkers? Watching her, waiting for another moment to grab her? Would she ever feel safe again?

THREE

"Make way!" Two volunteers squeezed through the front doors of the new, temporary homeless shelter carrying a leather couch, the last of the salvageable furniture from the old shelter.

Standing in the narrow entryway, Tim hooked an arm around Vickie's waist and drew her up against his chest while he tucked Frodo next to his leg.

She stiffened and glanced at him before quickly looking away. He kept his hold loose so as not to crush her, but had a hard time ignoring the awareness zinging through him from the close contact. She'd shed her jacket an hour ago as they'd worked to make the donated space habitable.

She barely reached his chin. Her blond hair hung loose about her shoulders, and though the lingering odor of the fire clung to her, there was a hint of sugar and apples in the silky strands teasing his senses.

He noticed one of the firefighters giving her the once-over and wanted to growl at him like a possessive dog with a bone. So not the way he should be feeling. But given someone had attacked her tonight, he decided he could be a bit territorial.

In a protective way, of course. Nothing personal. He wasn't looking for anything personal. He was content with his life. Adding in any kind of relationship would only complicate things. He didn't like complications.

Once the path was clear, he released his hold on her. She stepped away with a shy smile that packed a powerful punch. "Thanks."

"Anytime." He tugged on the collar of his uniform. "At least the heat is working in here."

She dropped her gaze to Frodo. "He's a handsome dog. May I pet him?"

"Of course."

She hesitated with her hand poised in the air. "He won't bite?"

"Not unless I command him to," Tim replied with a smile. "His specialty is arson investigations. He alerts on accelerants."

Tentatively, Vickie held her hand out for the German shepherd to sniff. Then crouching slightly to reach him, she ran her palm over his sleek head and rubbed him behind the ears. "You're a good boy." She looked at Tim. "How old is he?"

"He'll be three on New Year's Eve."

"How long have you had him?"

"The FBI purchased him when he was ten months old. We've been together for the past two years."

She straightened. "I'm thankful you and Frodo are here." She blinked as if surprised by the admission.

He struggled to suppress a chuckle. It wasn't

every day a pretty woman told him she was glad he was around and it wasn't contrived.

She leveled her shoulders and met his gaze. "It was amazing you were able to convince Mr. Johnson to open up the building for the shelter."

"Considering he'd latched on to the idea of letting the media know of his generosity, I think it's safe to say he realized the benefits of charity," Tim replied.

She laughed, the sound soft and pleasing. He liked it.

"I don't think it was a coincidence the building was empty," she said. "God arranged this. He knew we'd need it tonight."

Puzzled by her logic, he said, "But if God knew we'd need a new shelter, then why did He let the old one burn?"

"I wish I knew. God's ways are a mystery. But I have to believe everything happens for a reason even if we don't understand."

He mulled over her words. He believed in God and His son. Yet he'd seen so much evil and heartache through the years, he couldn't comprehend the point of it all. "I'm not sure I have that same level of faith."

"A little faith can grow."

He grinned. "Like a mustard seed."

She grinned back. "Exactly. Sunday school?"

"Vacation Bible school, actually."

"Me, too. Every summer. My favorite was the

summer I was ten. The theme was pirates. I still have my pirate hat. I was quite the scallywag." In the dim glow of the overhead lights Tim could see her cheeks turning pink.

He pictured her as a young girl sporting a tricorn hat with a feather plume and brandishing a rubber sword. Did she still have a playful side? So far he'd witnessed her stellar work ethic and her compassion and kindness toward others. She'd handled herself like a pro tonight with the media. He'd sensed her nervousness, but it hadn't shown as she'd recounted witnessing the blaze igniting.

"Here you are." Sasha Petrov emerged from the atrium. "Come inside. Pastor John wants to say a few words before we disperse."

They followed her father into the large open space in the center of the building where rows of cots dominated one side of the area, while tables and benches were in the center, and a few couches had been arranged in front of a television off to the other side of the room. Tim and Frodo stayed close to Vickie as they squeezed into the crowd.

"Thank you, everyone, for your help." Pastor John stood on a chair and addressed the many people who had come forward to help relocate the residents of the Billings Homeless Shelter.

The show of support from the community impressed Tim, especially those from Pastor John's congregation. As many as fifty families had arrived within a half hour of when the call for help had gone out.

"The Petrovs have offered to bring over Christmas sandwiches tomorrow. Let's give them a round of applause," Pastor John said.

Tim clapped and leaned close to Vickie to say, "Your family is very generous."

Her eyes glowed with delight. "My parents bake and cook. And feeding others is a joy to them. I think it's a perfect way to show God's love on Christmas Day."

He couldn't agree more. Too bad he'd be on duty tomorrow. But at least Vickie would be safe with her family. He'd make sure there was a police presence both at the bakery and at the shelter.

"Please go home and enjoy your families for Christmas," Pastor John said. "God bless you all and Merry Christmas."

Amid a chorus of Merry Christmases and chatter, the crowd dispersed. Tim placed his hand to the small of Vickie's back again and guided her and Frodo across the atrium to where her parents were gathered with Pastor John and Lacey Klems.

"Agent Ramsey, you're still here?" Irena said.

"Yes, ma'am," Tim replied. "I won't be allowed to inspect the fire scene until it's safe for us." Once the embers had cooled and there was no chance of a secondary flare-up, he and Frodo would search for the point of origin and the cause of the fire.

"We appreciate your work, Agent Ramsey," Sasha said, and held out his hand.

Clasping it firmly, Tim said, "Thank you, sir."

"Yes, we are grateful for your help tonight." Pastor John held out his hand in turn and Tim shook it.

"Please keep us informed on the progress you make in the investigation," Lacey said.

"I will, ma'am," Tim assured the shelter director. With a nod, she moved away with the pastor to say goodnight to more people.

Sasha put his arm around Irena. "Time to head home, my love. Morning will come faster than we'd like."

Irena addressed her daughter. "Coming, Vickie?"

"Yes. But I need to find my coat," she said. "I don't remember where I set it when we came in."

"You laid it on a chair in the entryway," Tim reminded her. Reluctance twisted in his stomach. He wasn't ready to see her walk out the door just yet. To her parents, he said, "I'll drive her home."

He told himself he was just doing his job. Protect and serve. Keeping a witness safe. All part of his duties as an officer of the law.

"Not necessary," Vickie said.

"Maybe not, but I'd like to make sure you arrive safely," he improvised. "And I can confirm that a Billings patrol officer is on guard."

"Thank you, Agent Ramsey," Irena said. "I trust you'll take good care of our daughter." She patted Vickie's arm with a gleam in her eyes. "We'll see you at home."

Vickie watched her parents leave before turning back to him. She tilted her head to the side. There was wariness in her eyes. "Are you always so attentive to victims of crimes?"

"When a witness is in danger," he told her. Though in truth, he rarely saw the people involved. He dealt with the evidence. The charred remains. "Until we catch the arsonist, you won't be safe."

Her face paled at the reminder. "Right. Because he doesn't know if I can identify him or not." They walked toward the entryway. "Maybe I should talk to the news people again and let them know for certain I didn't get a clear look at the man's face."

"We could do that," Tim told her. "But you may still be able to help us find him. We won't know for sure until you meet with Brian, the forensic artist."

Vickie stopped. The row of chairs lined against the wall were empty. They searched the building for it but to no avail. She sighed. "My coat's gone. Bummer. Maybe it will turn up later. Someone probably grabbed it by mistake."

Though Tim wasn't surprised someone had taken off with her coat with so many people coming and going from the place, he felt bad just the same. "Was there anything of value in the pockets?"

"No, thankfully. I left my purse and wallet with all my credit cards at home."

He took off his outer jacket. "You can wear mine."

"But you'll be cold," she protested.

"I'll be fine," he assured her. "Let's get you home."

He helped her into his jacket. She had to push the sleeves up at the elbows in order for her hands to come out of the sleeves. She pulled the collar up close and seemed to burrow into it with a sigh that sounded suspiciously like contentment, and it stirred a yearning inside him he didn't want to examine. Best to ignore any soft emotions right now.

They left the building and stepped into the quiet night. Snow blanketed the world in white but the sky was clear at the moment. There was no one around, only a few cars parked along the curb. He'd left his SUV in the lot of the building across the road.

The unmistakable sound of an engine turning over down the block echoed in the stillness, but no headlights came on.

Uneasiness slinked up his spine and settled in the muscles of his neck. He urged Vickie and Frodo across the street at a quick pace.

The squeal of tires on the slick pavement rent the air.

Frodo barked a warning.

A dark sedan pulled away from the curb and

barreled toward them, a hulking, inky shadow racing to take them down.

Releasing Frodo's lead, Tim shouted the command, "Sidewalk!"

Frodo immediately darted out of the road, freeing Tim to grab Vickie. He lifted her off her feet and tucked her into his chest as he dived out of the way, taking them both to the ground. He gritted his teeth as the sedan zoomed past them, barely missing their legs. Frodo's angry barks bounced off the icy pavement.

Sitting up quickly, Tim stared after the vehicle, straining to make out the license number in the glow of the taillights. The plate had been removed. Frustration churned in his gut.

Vickie righted herself but remained within the circle of his arms. "What just happened?"

His gut clenched with dread and anger. "Somebody tried to kill us."

"How can you be sure?" Her voice trembled and her body shook within his embrace. "Maybe the driver didn't see us."

"Maybe." Though he doubted that was the case. He shifted and winced.

"You're hurt!" She quickly disengaged herself from his arms. "We need to get you to the hospital."

Though he appreciated her concern, the only place they were going was to her home. He slowly rose, testing the various places that ached. "I'm just banged up. Nothing broken." He helped her to her feet. "Come on, we need to get off the street before that maniac decides to return."

"You can't know for sure he was trying to hurt us," she said.

She really didn't want to believe her life was in danger. Tim understood. He didn't have to be a mind reader to know she was a woman who saw the good in others. She had a sweet and gentle nature. He wished he could protect her from the reality of the situation but he couldn't. He was sure that car had intentionally tried to hit them. Though he could have been the target, he'd made enough enemies over the years, he was convinced the arsonist Vickie had seen had been behind the wheel.

"Either way, we're reporting the car," he said.

After helping her into his SUV and securing Frodo in his compartment, Tim called 911, identified himself and explained the situation to the dispatcher. They waited for the Billings Police Department to arrive and take their statements about the incident.

Then he drove Vickie to the Petrovs' home, keeping an alert eye out for the sedan. After circling the block to make sure they hadn't been followed, he pulled into the driveway of the two-story house on a tree-lined street. Colored Christmas lights hung from the eaves. A large decorative Christmas tree was showcased in the front window.

Tim was gratified to see a marked patrol car parked across the street. He walked Vickie to the porch. "You'll be safe tonight. If the officer sees anything suspicious, he'll call for backup."

"Thank you for all you've done for me," she said. The warm glow of the porch light shone on her hair, highlighting the blond strands.

"Just doing my job." He stared into her blue-gray eyes and realized he could easily lose himself in the stormy depths. So pretty and sweet.

She hesitated. "You probably have a family waiting for you at home, right?"

"No. No one." Was she fishing?

"No girlfriend expecting you to come by?" she pressed.

She *was* fishing. His ego puffed up a bit and lifted one corner of his mouth. "Not in a very long time."

As one of the only single agents left on the team, he'd opted to be on call tonight and on duty tomorrow, allowing all his teammates to enjoy the holiday with their loved ones. Seemed the least he could do, since he had no family to speak of. Only Frodo.

Standing here with Vickie, his body still humming with residual adrenaline, he couldn't say he regretted being on duty tonight.

Vickie tilted her head again. "What happened to her? Your girlfriend from a long time ago?"

"She moved on without me." He expected to

feel the old anger stir, but it didn't. Odd. And yet, looking at Vickie, it was hard for him to think of any other woman.

Vickie cleared her throat. "What about your parents?"

"My folks divorced when I was a kid." There'd been a time when the subject of his parents made bitterness well up. Now he felt only a sad resignation. He'd never have a close, loving relationship with his parents.

"I'm sorry," she said. "That must have been hard."

"It was. They each remarried and started new families. I bounced back and forth between them until I went away to college."

"That's rough," she murmured.

He shrugged. "It was a long time ago. Now my family is the team and Frodo."

"You could stay here with us." Her cheeks turned bright red beneath the porch light. "I mean, to have a late Christmas Eve dinner. You have to eat, right?" she added quickly.

He studied her. "What is up with you and Greg Sherman? He acted like you and he were involved."

She tucked in her chin. "We're not... Our relationship isn't like that. We're acquaintances at most. We went to grade school and high school together. I hadn't seen him in years until he took the job as security guard."

Tim couldn't believe how strangely relieved he was to hear her say that. It made no sense why he should care one way or the other. "He made it sound like there was more between you."

She huffed out an irritated sigh. "He'd like more. He keeps asking me out and I keep turning him down."

Motive to hurt her? Tim's heart rate ticked up. But why set the fire? "Do you think he could be the one who attacked you?"

She bit at her lip. "I considered it, but…"

"But?"

She hesitated, as if debating with herself, then she gave her head a sharp shake. "The man's face was in shadows. It happened so fast."

Acid burned in Tim's gut. Had he let the arsonist walk away? "Do you know what kind of car Greg drives?"

"No, I don't. He's always walking when he comes into the bakery."

"I'll look into Greg. See if he has an alibi." Not just for tonight, but for each fire. "When you work with the forensic artist we'll have a better idea of whether you saw the man's face or not. The subconscious can reveal a lot even when we don't think we've seen anything."

"I hope that's true," she said with a tremble in her voice. "I really want this creep caught."

"Me, too. We'll get him." Tim wouldn't rest until the man responsible for trying to hurt

Vickie and burning up much of the city was brought to justice.

"You didn't answer my question. Will you stay?"

The desire to say yes welled up, making his chest tight. As much as he'd like to spend time with Vickie and her parents, he had a job to do.

The eager expectancy in her face undid him. What was it about this woman that made him want to please her?

He glanced up, seeking help from above, and discovered a sprig of mistletoe hanging over the porch. Uh-oh.

Time to retreat before he did something he'd regret, like kiss her.

FOUR

A simple yes or no would suffice. Vickie didn't understand why Tim wasn't responding to her invitation to come inside for a late dinner.

He stared at the porch ceiling, his face losing its color. She glanced up to see what had affected him so adversely.

A mistletoe ball entwined with red and silver ribbons hung over their heads.

Her stomach clenched with a burst of alarm. She reared back, stumbling against the closed front door. Clearly, she wasn't as good at containing her reaction to the mistletoe as Tim.

Why, oh why, did her dad insist on putting that thing there every year?

She knew exactly why. So he had an extra excuse to kiss her mother every time they crossed the threshold. After thirty years of marriage, her dad was still a hopeless romantic.

In the chaos of the evening, Vickie had completely forgotten about the offending plant taunting her each time she entered and left the house. No wonder poor Tim blanched and now quickly edged backward toward the steps, hoping to make a speedy exit. She didn't blame him. Being trapped into a silly tradition of kissing beneath the green decoration wasn't her idea of a good time. And apparently not Tim's, either.

"Never mind about dinner," she said, willing to let him off the hook so they could both escape the embarrassment of not wanting to share a kiss, despite the uncomfortable burn of disappointment leaching through her. "You have work to do. You should go. I'm sure your dog needs you."

Now my family is the team and Frodo. The thought of him alone with only his dog as a companion made her want to hug him. A reaction she really shouldn't be having about him.

He smiled slightly. "Yes. I should go. Work. Fire." He stepped down the first stair. "I'll see you tomorrow."

She couldn't help the tiny thrill to know she'd see him the next day. She clamped her mouth shut. Silly. He meant when she worked with the forensic artist. He obviously wasn't interested in her on a personal level.

The thought depressed her, which was totally ridiculous. She wasn't interested in him, either, regardless of how handsome and kind she found him, which could all be an illusion designed to trick her. She wouldn't be taken in again by a chiseled jaw and thoughtfulness.

"Good night." She fled inside and closed the door with a snap, then let out a breath. Her knees felt shaky. It was the residual adrenaline from the day, not because of Tim. *Yeah, sure.*

"Vickie?" her mother called from the kitchen. The delicious aroma of her traditional borscht soup, made from beets, broth and a host of winter vegetables, filled the house.

"Yes, Mom. Coming." She decided she'd not tell her parents about the car incident. No need to worry them unduly.

Besides, she wasn't sure the vehicle had been aiming for them. Maybe the person behind the wheel had been drunk or hadn't seen her and Tim. There had to be another explanation other than someone trying to kill them. Despite her reasoning, a tremor of apprehension skated across her skin.

She could only pray that tomorrow she'd be able to give a detailed enough description of the man who'd attacked her and started the homeless shelter fire.

And tried to run her and Tim down.

She had to trust Tim would succeed in capturing the villain.

Maybe this time justice wouldn't fail her.

Tim and Frodo returned to the remains of the Billings Homeless Shelter fire. The temperature had dropped and more snow fell from the sky, making the scene a soupy mess. Kind of how Tim felt.

When he'd glanced up and spotted the mistletoe hanging from the porch over him and Vickie, the thought of kissing Vickie had taken hold of his imagination and shook it until the yearning to kiss her had been overwhelming.

He'd barely managed to retreat before giving in. And judging from the way Vickie had reacted once she'd realized they were standing beneath the decoration, she wouldn't have been amenable to fulfilling the Christmas tradition.

Which was good. For them both.

With effort, he put Vickie and his scattered feelings about her aside as he donned gloves and booties for him and Frodo before releasing the dog from the SUV and grabbing his evidence collection kit.

The fire chief and several other firefighters were still on scene, wrapping up their hoses and gathering other equipment.

"Chief," Tim said in greeting.

"Agent Ramsey, good timing," Clark replied. "The fire's cold." He rolled his neck as if to relieve his tension. "It's a wonder the whole building wasn't consumed. But thankfully, the call to dispatch came quickly." The chief gestured to the blackened remains. "You two can do your thing. Let me know what you find."

"Yes, sir." To Frodo, Tim said, "Seek." The cue word was to let the dog know they were going to work now.

Tim and Frodo picked their way through the rubble of ash and debris covered in snow to the back door of the shelter and the Dumpster. Vickie had stated the fire had started in this area. The scorch pattern from the ground behind the Dumpster and up the side of the building was odd.

Not like the three arson cases he'd worked this month. Maybe they were dealing with a different perpetrator.

He poked around the rubble, not finding anything of note. Frodo sniffed the edges of the Dumpster and let out a loud bark, then sat at attention.

Tim squatted down to see what had the dog alerting. Beneath the back edge of the Dumpster were remnants of a matchbook and a tiny portion of a cigarette filter. Okay.

Tim's heart rate kicked up. So the same method of combustion was used, but why had it burned hotter and faster?

He bagged the evidence, placed a marker in the spot with a number to correspond to the evidence bag, and stood to stare at the structure, taking in the unusual burn pattern. Definitely some sort of accelerant had been used, but not gasoline this time.

"Good job, Frodo."

The dog let out a quick bark in response to the praise. Then he set his nose to the ground and sniffed. Tim let out the German shepherd's lead, letting him explore a wider diameter of the cordoned-off area. Frodo halted a few feet away, then sat, once again alerting to something on the ground. Tim hurried over to inspect his find.

A dark glob on the pavement had drawn Frodo's attention.

Using a small chisel from his tool kit, Tim pried the substance free to allow for examination. Though the crime lab would confirm his analysis, he knew without a doubt that he was looking at a drop of a highly flammable type of petroleum wax. The accelerant used in this fire. He slipped the substance into a pint-size arson evidence solid material collection container and marked the spot on the ground.

His educated guess would be the arsonist had coated the back wall of the shelter with the wax and left a trail to the matchbook, so that when the cigarette burned down and the matches ignited, the wax caught fire. Tim told the chief and his men as much.

"Clever and dangerous," the chief said. "We've got to catch this guy."

A murmur of agreement went through the group.

"Our witness is set to work with a forensic artist," Tim told them. "The FBI will be operating closely with the Billings police department."

And if all went well, they'd have their arsonist by the New Year.

Christmas morning dawned with a clear sky and the world carpeted in pristine white snow. Vickie glanced out her bedroom window overlooking the neighborhood, enjoying the peaceful serenity of the quiet street and the festively decorated homes. A few chimneys had plumes of smoke spiraling into the air, signaling that the day had already begun in many households.

The only thing marring the postcard-like scene was the police cruiser sitting across the street from her house.

She expected the sight to make her uneasy, scared, but having the police officer present was a reminder Tim had kept his promise of making sure she and her family were protected. That they were safe.

She turned away from the window. Normally on Christmas morning she'd head downstairs in her pajamas to have breakfast with her parents. But today she dressed with care, because she would be seeing Tim.

And the forensic artist. To catch a criminal.

Seeing Tim wasn't a big deal and not why she'd chosen her new green sweater. As she applied a touch of lipstick, she made a face at herself in the vanity mirror. "Get over yourself."

The sound of the doorbell sent her heart rate skipping.

A few moments later her mother opened the bedroom door to say, "Agent Ramsey and his dog are here. Looking very handsome. The agent, that is." She laughed. "The dog, too, actually. You should invite Agent Ramsey to breakfast."

"I doubt he'll have time for breakfast."

"Are you all right? You look a bit pale."

Vickie waved away her mother's concern. "I'm fine. I just didn't sleep well." Not to mention how nervous she was to recreate a mental image of her attacker. She prayed she could give enough of a description for Tim to arrest him.

Taking her hand, her mom drew her close. "That's understandable. Yesterday was traumatic. But today is Christmas Day. A day of new beginnings."

Vickie wanted to believe she had the chance to begin again; however, she wouldn't feel safe until the police caught the man responsible for the fire. The man who had attacked her and then possibly tried to run her down. Though she wasn't convinced the car incident had been intentional. But Tim was. And she trusted him to know. It was his job, after all. To know things like that.

Not wanting to cause her mother any more worry, Vickie suppressed a shiver and took a calming breath. She'd become stronger over the past few years. She would get through this.

Her mom tugged her hand. "Come along. You don't want to keep your young man waiting."

Vickie groaned. "He's not my young man, Mom. Please don't say things like that in front of Agent Ramsey."

Irena grinned. "Touchy, touchy."

Holding on to her composure, Vickie followed

her downstairs. Tim and her father were in the living room, talking. Both men turned as they entered. Vickie's heart gave a little knock against her ribs at the sight of the handsome agent. His brown hair flopped over his forehead in a cute way that made her want to reach out and brush it back. Her fingers curled at her sides.

He wore civilian clothes—dark wash jeans, a button-down plaid shirt beneath a warm, shearling-lined leather jacket. He held a small wrapped box in his hands. For her?

Swallowing back the sudden delight, she dropped her gaze. At Tim's booted feet lay his muscular German shepherd. The dog stared at her with dark, intelligent eyes. The pair made a striking picture.

Tim smiled and his blue eyes glowed with appreciation. "Good morning, Vickie. Merry Christmas."

Heat flushed through her cheeks. "Merry Christmas."

He extended the gift. "This was on your porch. It had your name on it." He frowned. "The patrol officer didn't see anyone drop it off, so it must have been there from before you returned home last night and we hadn't noticed."

Disappointment surged and she fought the emotion back. Of course he wasn't bringing her a present. She stared at the package. Who would leave her a gift? And why?

"Well, open it," her father said. "Maybe there's a card inside."

"Ooh, a mysterious admirer," her mother quipped.

Reluctantly, Vickie took the package and carefully unwrapped the festive paper to reveal a black box. She lifted the lid. A small gold cross on a delicate chain lay nestled in the batting. Her hand trembled. Her mind rebelled. It couldn't be. She forced herself not to flinch.

"That's pretty. You used to have a cross like that when you were in college," her mother said. "Whatever happened to it?"

"I lost it." She'd realized she was missing her cross the day after Ken assaulted her. She'd figured it had come off during the struggle, but she hadn't found it in the apartment. Then she'd packed up and returned home, never thinking about the necklace again.

"Is there a note?" Tim asked.

"No. No note." She slammed the lid shut and met his concerned gaze. Now was not the time or place for her to discuss the past. No matter how distressing she found the gift. "Shouldn't we go?"

His gaze never wavered. "Brian, the forensic artist, won't be available until tomorrow."

The news was both a relief and a disappointment. She wanted to get this part over with, but now, with this box in her hand making her skin crawl with anxiety, she wanted nothing more than to hole up inside her parents' house and forget the past existed. "You could have called to tell me."

Tugging at the collar of his shirt, he said, "I could have. But I thought it would be better for me to tell you in person."

Interesting. And a bit disconcerting. Was he attracted to her, too? The thought left her feeling unbalanced. Or was that caused only by the box in her hand. "Thank you."

Her mom nudged her in the side. *Oh, right. Breakfast.* "Would you like to stay for Christmas breakfast?"

Tim hesitated a fraction of a second before he nodded. "I'd like that very much."

Warmth spread through her chest. She would, too. "Good." She set the little black box on the mantel, glad to not be touching it. If only she could put it from her mind as easily. "Here, let me take your coat."

He slipped his outerwear from his wide shoulders and handed it to her. The jacket retained his body heat and a faint spicy aroma.

Her father clapped Tim on the back. "We can't thank you enough for your help yesterday."

"All part of the job," Tim replied, his gaze on her.

Feeling as though he could see right through her to the hidden torment bubbling inside, Vickie headed toward the hall closet to hang up his outerwear. She held it to her chest for a moment and again breathed in the lingering scent of Tim's aftershave clinging to the leather collar. The material was so warm and inviting. She had the strongest urge to slip the jacket around her, as if doing so would keep her safe.

The sight of the cross necklace loomed in her mind like a neon sign. Her hands tightened, bunching up Tim's coat. Who sent it? Why? She wanted to believe it was a benevolent gift, but she couldn't shake the alarming feeling the present held more malice than goodwill.

Quickly, she grabbed a hanger and hung up the coat. Security wouldn't be found in a coat or in the arms of an attractive FBI agent.

The scuff of a shoe on the hardwood floor sent Vickie's heart jumping. She spun from the closet door, her fists raised high so that her forearms protected her face.

"Whoa!" Tim said, his hands held up, his palms facing her. "I didn't mean to startle you."

Recapturing the breath that had leaped out of her, Vickie lowered her arms and tried to school her features into a neutral expression. "You didn't."

He cocked an eyebrow. "Right."

Caught. She sighed. "I'm a little jumpy."

"Understandable, given the circumstances of the past twelve hours."

He had no idea. The necklace was a reminder of a time in her life she'd worked so hard to forget.

"Thank you for keeping your promise of a police presence last night."

A hard glint entered his blue eyes. "You'll have protection until we catch this guy."

Such a different response than she'd received from the police when she'd reported Ken's assault. "We appreciate your care."

"You'll have a police escort any time you leave the house. I don't want to take any chances the guy in the car makes another attempt to run you down."

Her stomach lurched at the reminder. She glanced toward the kitchen, where her parents were busy putting the last touches on their Christmas breakfast. "Shh. I didn't tell my parents about that."

His eyes widened. "I'm surprised. I thought you and your parents were close."

"We are," she told him in a fierce voice. "I love them beyond measure. Which is why I need to protect them."

"They should know what's happening," he insisted.

"It could have easily been an accident. Or you could have been the intended target." The skepticism and resolved gleam in his eyes told her he wasn't buying her rationale. "But even if that car meant to mow me down, why make my parents worry about something they can't do anything about?" She touched his arm. "Please. I don't want to upset them any more than I have to."

He shook his head in clear disapproval and stared at her for several moments.

She entwined her fingers together, waiting for him to either argue with her or flat out ignore her plea.

Finally, he stilled and narrowed his gaze. "It's your call."

She blinked in surprise. It took her a moment to recover. She hadn't expected him to acquiesce so easily. Men in authority, like him, usually wanted to be in control. Nevertheless, she was grateful he understood. She squeezed his arm. "Thank you."

"For now," he amended. "If anything else happens, you'll need to let them know. They would be devastated if you ended up hurt."

His words rang ominously between them. Anxiety ate at her gut. He was right, of course, which was why she would do everything in her power to keep them all from being hurt.

"Tell me about the necklace," Tim said. "It upset you. Why?"

"It's creepy that someone would leave it on the porch," she stated.

"I agree, but there's something more, because your face lost all of its color the second you opened the box and saw what was inside."

Her uncontrollable response had betrayed her. How could she tell Tim about Ken? Would he dismiss her claim of being attacked, as everyone else had? "I was surprised. Why would someone send me a gift and not leave a note with it?"

"Like your mother said, a secret admirer?" His eyebrows rose. "Or maybe not-so-secret. Greg?"

The thought had merit. She was panicking for nothing. Of course the necklace was from Greg. "But why a cross?"

"Because anyone who knows you knows you are a person of faith," Tim said.

She supposed he was right. There was no reason for her to read more into the gold charm and chain than a nice gesture. "Why would Greg leave it on the porch? He came to the shelter last night."

"Maybe he came by here before going to the shelter," Tim reasoned. "I'll find out. You don't have to worry. I'll take care of it."

His determination and thoughtfulness endeared him to her even more than he already was—which scared her nearly as much as knowing there was a serial arsonist out there who wanted to silence her.

FIVE

Tim sat at the square table in the Petrovs' dining room with Vickie on his right, looking beautiful in green, with her blond hair loose about her shoulders. He couldn't help but notice how she fidgeted in her seat.

He only wished there was some way for him to ease Vickie's worry. Arresting the maniac would make her feel safe. Make them all feel safe.

The unsigned gift was a concern, but Tim was sure Greg was the sender. The man had made it clear he thought he had a claim on Vickie.

Not likely. She was too good for Greg. Too good for Tim, too, for that matter. She deserved someone well-adjusted and willing to give everything to her. That wasn't Tim. He'd tried going all in before with disastrous results. He wasn't willing to try again.

The other seats at the table were taken by Irena and Sasha. Frodo lay near the back door, his head resting on his crossed paws.

The delicious breakfast of sweet rolls with raspberry jam and butter, poached eggs and sausage, along with potato dumplings, would keep Tim going all day and into the next. But it was the lively conversation and the comfortable way the Petrov family welcomed him and Frodo into their home that filled him with yearning.

He couldn't remember the last time he'd had a home-cooked meal that didn't involve one or more of his fellow agents. The Tactical K-9 Unit members were as close as he came to having family, but sitting here with Vickie and her parents stirred a need to belong to something more. To *someone* more.

His chest tightened. He knew from painful experience what happened when he let down his guard and gave in to the need for more. Heartbreak waited at the end that path. A path he wouldn't travel again.

Sasha stretched. "As always, my dear, scrumptious."

Irena touched her husband's arm with a loving smile. "I'm glad you enjoyed your breakfast. Now you may help with the dishes." She rose and gathered the empty plates and took them to the sink in the kitchen.

Sasha pushed back his chair. "Vickie, why don't you and Tim visit in the living room while your mother and I deal with the cleanup?"

Tim stood. "I can help."

Sasha waved him off. "You're our guest. Please. This won't take long. Then we can play a game or two before we head to the bakery. We're going to provide food for the homeless shelter again."

The thought of staying with the Petrovs for merriment and serving the people staying at the shelter appealed to Tim, but he was scheduled to work. "I can't stay. I'm on duty again today. I need to get to headquarters." He'd make sure an officer stayed close to the family all day.

"Isn't today a federal holiday?" Vickie asked.

"It is, but someone needs to be available to take any calls that come in," Tim told her. "I'm due to relieve the morning shift."

Sasha stuck out his hand. "Ah. Well, I wish you a Merry Christmas then."

Tim shook his hand. He liked the older gentleman. "Thank you, sir. Merry Christmas to you, as well."

Irena returned to the dining table and linked her arm through her husband's. "Thank you for taking time to spend with us this morning."

"My pleasure," Tim replied. "This was the best Christmas breakfast I've ever eaten."

Irena beamed. "That's so sweet of you to say." She turned to Vickie. "Offer our guest some chocolate to take with him."

"Yes, Mom." Vickie rose and gestured for him to follow her to the living room.

He whistled and Frodo jumped to his feet. They followed her.

Tim had noticed the large decorated tree showcased in front of the bay windows, and liked the colorful ornaments. And the three Christmas stockings hanging above the gas fireplace from gold-plated mantel holders that spelled out the word *joy*.

The room was cozy and festive, just as a home should be at Christmas. He liked it. His apartment had no decorations, no tree and certainly no stocking waiting for treats.

"Do you always work the holidays?" Vickie asked. She went to the tree and plucked a small wrapped gift from a branch.

"Usually," he said. "That way the others who have family can spend time with their loved ones."

She stopped in front of him. "It makes me sad to think of you alone at Christmas."

He appreciated her concern. "I'm not alone. I have Frodo."

"That's an interesting name to choose for your partner," she commented. "A fan of Tolkien?"

"Yes. Very much so. Frodo was brave and determined. Qualities I saw in this guy when I met him," Tim said, with a glance at the dog sitting beside him.

Vickie held out the present. "This chocolate comes from the Ukraine. My parents have it shipped over every year, and we give a box to those we care about."

He closed his hand around the gift and her warm, slender fingers. "I'm honored to be included in the category of people you care about."

A blush tinged her cheeks. She slipped her hand away. "After all you did for us and the homeless shelter yesterday, you'll receive chocolate every year."

He held her gaze. "I do love chocolate."

"It's good for the heart."

Though he knew she meant physically healthy, he couldn't help the way her words wound around him, making him want to open his heart to her. A dangerous idea that wouldn't serve him well. He wasn't looking for romance. She was a victim of a crime and it was his job to protect her. Nothing more. He didn't need to be with her to make sure she was protected, no matter how much he enjoyed spending time with her.

Yet he found himself saying, "When you head to the shelter, let me know. I'll come help you."

Her eyes widened. "That would be lovely. Thank you."

She opened the front door.

They both glanced up at the decorative ball of mistletoe hanging from the porch eave, then their gazes met and held for a moment before they both grinned.

"My dad's doing," she said. "He and Mom are hopeless romantics."

A chuckle escaped him. The Petrovs were a charming family. Especially Vickie. "I'll see you later." He ducked out the door, careful to skirt around the mistletoe and moved quickly across the porch. No need to stop and linger even if he'd like to.

Later that afternoon at the bakery, Vickie finished packing the last box of food ready to be taken to the temporary homeless shelter. Slipping into her father's office, she called the number Tim had given her for his cell phone. Her heart beat in her ears as she waited for him to answer, eager to hear his voice.

His voice mail picked up. She kept her disappointment in check as she left a message that she was heading to the shelter.

When she stepped out of the office, her mom was checking on the fruit pies in the oven. "These have another fifteen minutes or so to go."

Vickie glanced at the clock on the wall. Four thirty. "We told Pastor John we'd be there at five. How about I take over the boxes and you and Dad can bring the pies when they're ready to be transported?"

Concern darkened her mother's eyes. "We all came together. How will you get to the shelter?"

"I'll ask Officer Reeves to drive me."

Tim had made good, once again, on his promise of making sure they had a guard to keep them safe. Officer Reeves sat in the dining area enjoying her mom's coffee cake. He was a rookie with the Billings police department and very nice. He readily agreed to accompany Vickie to the shelter.

Bundled for the cold, Vickie and the policeman left the bakery in his patrol car, then had to park on the other side of the snowed-covered grass because the plows had pushed all the snow to the sides of the street, blocking the parking spaces.

The crunch of their booted feet on the salt-covered sidewalk masked the sound of the surprising amount of traffic on the roads, considering it was Christmas Day.

"Thank you for helping me with these," Vickie said, nodding toward the box in Officer Reeves's hands, while she adjusted the one she carried.

"No problem," he replied. His held condiments and two containers filled with her mom's potato salad. "The fresh air is good for the soul." He grinned. "At least that is what my grandmother always tells me."

"Wise words." Vickie adjusted her grip on the box filled with sweet rolls, savory rolls, sandwich breads and an array of deli meats and cheeses.

A slither of sensation along her nape raised the fine hairs at the base of her skull. She glanced behind her. No one was there.

Paranoid much? she asked herself. She studied the cars passing by on the street, remembering the squeal of tires when the dark sedan had tried to run her and Tim down.

"It would be shorter cutting across the community park than staying on the sidewalk," Vickie said, as they neared the corner where the street diverged around the tree-filled green space.

The sense of being watched shivered across her flesh, again urging her to move quickly into the park. Officer Reeves marched along a few paces behind her.

An odd sound had her glancing back to ask if he was okay, but the words died on her tongue. The officer was face-first in the snow, the box he'd been carrying beside him. Had he fallen?

She spun awkwardly, intending to rush to his aid, but was stopped by hands clamping down on her shoulders and dragging her backward. She dropped the box in her arms as a wave of fear crashed into her, stealing her breath.

Jerking and twisting in an effort to free herself, she jabbed her elbows backward, but her assailant kept out of reach. An arm wrapped around her neck, pressing painfully against her throat.

A male voice hissed into her ear, "You'll pay for talking to the cops."

Clawing at the arm choking her, she tried to make sense of his words. *Pay?* "Please! Let me go."

Panic fueled by adrenaline infused her. She couldn't be a victim. Not again.

Save me, Lord.

She kicked backward and tore at the arm holding her. Her attacker lifted her off her feet and slammed her to the ground, burying her face into the snow. Icy wetness stung her cheeks and slipped beneath the collar of her coat. She kicked and punched as best she could, but the lack of oxygen caused the world to swim and fade. She was being choked and smothered.

Please, Lord, I don't want to die like this.

From a distance she heard a dog's furious barking.

Spots danced before her eyes. Her lungs ached. Terror ripped at her mind. She despaired of ever seeing Tim or her parents again as the world went dark.

SIX

Horror electrified Tim's blood as he brought his SUV to a screeching halt at the curb beside the community park. A man wearing a black hoodie and ski mask had Vickie on the ground in a choke-hold.

Using the fob on his key chain, Tim popped open Frodo's compartment. The dog bolted from the vehicle and sprinted forward in a burst of muscle and ferocious barking.

The assailant shot to his feet and ran in the opposite direction.

Tim jumped from his SUV. Heart hammering in his chest, he raced through the snow. "Halt! FBI!"

Frodo leaped in the air and bit down on the man's arm. The suspect let out a howl of pain, then twisted out of the jacket he wore, leaving Frodo with a mouthful of material. The dog spat it out and resumed his chase, easily gaining on the perpetrator.

When the assailant darted into the street, running directly into the path of the traffic, Tim feared for his partner's safety and gave a sharp whistle. Frodo wheeled around and raced back to his side.

Using his cell phone to call the Billings police

department, Tim quickly gave the dispatcher the suspect's description and requested an ambulance.

Tim checked the fallen officer for signs of life and was grateful to feel a pulse. A bloodied gash marred the back of the young man's head. A heavy-duty flashlight with blood on it lay next to him.

Next, Tim hurried to Vickie's side. She stirred as he gathered her in his arms. He brushed back a clump of wet, matted hair from her forehead, where a red knot was forming.

She blinked up at him as if she didn't trust what she was seeing. "You're here."

"I'm so sorry," he said. "I shouldn't have left your side."

"Not your fault." She struggled to stand. He helped her to her feet, tucking her into his side. She rubbed at her throat. "He came out of nowhere." Her eyes widened with alarm. "Officer Reeves?"

"Breathing. He took a nasty conk on the back of the head," Tim told her. "Help is on the way." A siren punctuated his words. "Did the attacker say anything?"

Fear clouded her eyes. "He said, 'You'll pay for talking to the cops.'"

"He *is* afraid you can identify him."

A tremble worked over her body. "I can't believe this is happening to me."

He hugged her closer in reassurance. He couldn't

help it. "The arsonist is determined to get away with his crimes. You're the only witness who can put him behind bars."

She bit her lip. "But how can you be certain it was him?"

Tim met her gaze. "Is there a reason to think there is someone else out there who wants to hurt you?"

Distress flickered in her eyes before she looked away. "I don't think so."

She didn't sound convincing. "What aren't you telling me?"

Before she could answer, officers and an ambulance were on scene. He reluctantly released her to the EMTs' care. They sat her on the bumper of the ambulance while they checked her head and neck, determining the damage was superficial. He hovered close, unwilling to let her out of his reach.

What was wrong with him?

He gave himself a mental shake. He needed to snap out of it.

Officer Reeves was placed on a gurney. He'd regained consciousness.

"I'm sorry, Agent Ramsey," he said. "I never saw him coming."

"We'll get him," Tim promised the younger man, as the paramedics wheeled him to the ambulance and took him to the hospital.

Tim turned back to Vickie as Police Chief Fielding approached.

Grasping Vickie's hand as she recounted the harrowing incident to the chief, Tim admired her strength and fortitude in the face of such a horrible experience.

He sent up a prayer of thanksgiving that he and Frodo had arrived in time to stop the assailant from doing permanent damage. The thought of losing Vickie sent Tim's pulse skyrocketing. He chose not to analyze the meaning beyond the knowledge that he'd come to care for her.

When Chief Fielding released them from the scene, telling Vickie investigators might contact her and Tim later with more questions, Tim helped her into his SUV. He then gathered the spilled contents of the two boxes and arranged for another Billings police officer to deliver the food to the shelter.

After he climbed into the driver's seat, he handed Vickie his phone. "Call your parents. Let them know what happened and that you are all right."

She made a face, but took the phone. "They are going to freak out."

"This is a freaky situation," he reminded her.

"True." She dialed. A few moments later she had them on the phone. As he listened to her calmly explain what had happened, he was struck once again by how very much he respected this sweet woman. She had a core of steel, but was also vulnerable and kind. She tried so hard to keep everyone around her comfortable, often to her own detriment.

When she clicked off and passed back his phone, he impulsively took her hand. "It's okay to be afraid. To ask for help and to let others be strong."

She laced her fingers through his. Surprise jolted Tim. Not only was Vickie accepting his touch after being physically attacked, but she was reciprocating. Her show of apparent trust in him sent warmth flooding through his chest.

"I don't want to be a burden on anyone."

His gaze dropped involuntarily to her lips. "You could never be." Why did his voice sound husky?

"Thank you."

He lifted his gaze to her trusting eyes. He wanted to say it was all part of the job, but somewhere along the way she'd become more than a job. "Let's get you home."

"Sounds good to me," she said.

On the drive to her house, Vickie was silent. Tim could only imagine how hard this was on her. She was being brave and stoic and he wanted to pull her into his arms and kiss away the little worry lines around her mouth and at the corners of her pretty eyes. He was in such deep water.

"If you and Frodo…" She hesitated, then shuddered as he brought the SUV to a halt in the driveway of her family home. "That man tried to kill me."

Battling back his own terror at how close the suspect had come to achieving his goal, Tim turned off the engine and gripped the steering wheel tight. "He didn't succeed. And he won't."

"How can you be so sure?"

"I just am." He had to believe he could stop this criminal before he hurt her or anyone else. He noted the police cruiser parked on the other side of the road with a clear view of the street.

Tim climbed out of the vehicle and came around to her side just as she stepped out. She swayed slightly as if the blood had rushed from her head. He wrapped an arm around her waist and was gratified when she leaned into him. He released Frodo, who did a quick sweep of the yard before joining them on the porch.

As Vickie unlocked the front door, Tim glanced up at the ball of mistletoe.

He couldn't stop himself from impulsively leaning close and placing a gentle kiss on her honey-blond hair.

She stilled and then slowly turned her face toward him. Her eyes were huge with obvious surprise and her lips parted on an inhaled breath.

He smiled and pointed up. "I couldn't resist."

She smiled softly. "Silly tradition."

"But a nice one," he replied, and reached past her to open the door.

A flush of pink heightened the color of her cheeks as she stepped inside the house. He and

Frodo followed. Frodo settled himself on the threshold of the living room.

Vickie moved to the gas fireplace and hit the switch, igniting a warming flame. She stood in front of the mantel, hugging her arms around her middle as she stared into the dancing fire with an unfocused gaze.

"Vickie, we'll catch him, I promise you."

She turned to face him. "I want to believe that. It's just…" She tugged on her bottom lip with her teeth.

For a moment he was distracted, wanting to take her in his arms and kiss away whatever was causing her to abuse her lip. "It's just what? You can tell me."

"It was a long time ago," she said, her voice sounding so fragile.

He frowned with unease and moved closer, but kept his hands at his sides, afraid he'd spook her. "Let me help," he coaxed in a gentle tone.

She pulled in a shuddering breath and spoke on her exhalation. "During my third year of college," she said, her voice barely above a whisper, "I was assaulted by the guy I was dating."

Tim's heart clutched. Anger on her behalf exploded within his chest. "Did he —?"

She shook her head. "No. But that was his intent."

His fingers curled at his sides. "Did you report the assault?"

"Yes." A grim light entered her eyes. "But no one believed me. It was his word against mine. And because he didn't actually succeed at what he wanted to do, there was *'no harm done.'*" She made air quotes with her fingers and a scoffing sound. "At least that was what the campus police and the school dean told me."

Outraged, Tim shook his head. "That shouldn't have happened."

Her smile broke his heart for its bitterness. "Doesn't matter now. I left school and never saw him again."

"What was his name?"

"Ken Leland. He was a big man on campus. Set to graduate with honors." Her shoulders wilted. "I shouldn't have gone out with him. The local police were willing to investigate when I went to them. They questioned Ken." She let out a bitter laugh. "But whatever he'd said to them had the officers insinuating I'd led Ken on and he'd misunderstood my intentions."

"It sounds like he was good at manipulation. Don't blame yourself," he said. "Not everyone is who they seem, but many are. All you can ever do is pray you're making the best decision you can and then trust God has your back."

"Do you really believe that?"

He searched his heart before finally answering. "Yes. There are times when I've had a split second to make a choice that could end or save a life, usually my own or Frodo's. I do the best I can and leave the rest to God."

Her gaze turned contemplative. "When I think back on that night, I can see God did intervene. My roommate came home, which forced Ken to escape out the back. I just wish I hadn't had to go through the rest."

"God doesn't always keep us from the bad things in life, but He does promise to be there with us." The words came out of some long-ago Sunday school lesson. He could apply those words to his own life, he realized with a start. Having his family torn apart and ripped out from under him as a kid had left scars, but God had never abandoned him, even if he felt abandoned.

The soft look of affection on her face made his stomach clench. "Thank you. I needed to hear that."

So had he. He reached for her hand and held her gaze. "Sometimes we need to be reminded of God's love and power."

The front door opened and her parents rushed inside, forcing him to release her and step back.

Her mother hurried to her side and embraced her. "Are you okay? We couldn't believe it when we heard you'd been assaulted on your way to the shelter."

"I'm fine, Mom," she told them. "Some bruises. Thankfully, Tim and Frodo saved me."

Sasha engulfed her in a hug, then turned to

Tim. "We owe you another debt of gratitude, Agent Ramsey."

"Not at all, sir." He wouldn't tell the man that protecting Vickie was something he longed to do forever. But acknowledging his budding feelings for her was a mistake he couldn't afford. He didn't need to be tangling up their lives and hearts amid such chaos. The forced proximity and heightened emotions weren't the foundations to build a romance on. Even if he wanted to. Which he didn't. Right?

"Tim, would you please stay for dinner?" Vickie asked, her eyes soft with pleading.

There was no way he could refuse her even if he wanted to. He needed to stay close to her because the arsonist had escalated to an attempted murderer. This was work. Nothing personal about it.

The next morning, Vickie and her parents opened the bakery as they did every day. Only today, Vickie's nerves were on edge as she readied the front of the store for the day's customers. A new police officer was stationed in the dining area. His presence eased some of her tension, but sleep had been elusive last night. Her mind had wanted to replay the assault every time she closed her eyes. Fatigue and worry were a combustible combination.

To distract herself from the trauma, she concentrated on Tim. On his kindness, his strength and integrity. So much different than she'd expected, considering he was an officer of the law. She realized now how silly she'd been assuming all those in authority were like the school dean and campus officer who'd made her feel small and worthless when she'd reported Ken's assault.

Tim was good and fair and full of honor. He made her feel safe and cared for. Cherished even. But did she dare risk opening her heart to him? The question made a different kind of tension form a knot in her chest.

The bell over the entrance door chimed when Tim stepped into the shop, and her heart leaped with the urge to rush into his arms. He looked handsome in khaki pants and a thick, warm-looking jacket with the FBI logo on the breast pocket. She wanted to believe he could keep her safe, but doubts swirled around her like wisps of smoke.

She wiped her trembling hands on the apron covering her jeans and shirt. "Good morning. Where's Frodo?"

"Good morning to you, too. He's sitting out front." Tim leaned against the counter. "Is this an okay time for you to take a break and come to headquarters with me? Brian's all set up and waiting."

She swallowed hard. Anxiety twisted her insides into knots. "I didn't see the man's face the night of fire. And yesterday, as you saw, he had a mask on. He came at me from behind."

Tim gathered her hands in his larger ones. Warmth spread up her arms, wrapping around her. She wanted to step away, to deny how much she needed his strength, but her feet and her heart wouldn't cooperate. "You said you'd caught a glimpse of him. You might have caught a glimpse of his eyes. The shape of his face. You'd be surprised by how much can be gleaned from that."

"I don't know how much more of this I can take."

He pulled her close. Surprise washed over her as she instinctively stiffened, expecting fear and panic to flood her. Ever since Ken's assault, she didn't like to be touched or hugged by anyone besides her parents. Strangely, within the circle of Tim's embrace, she found solace. With a sigh, she melted against him.

"You're doing great," he said, his voice rumbling in his chest. "I'm not going to let anything happen to you. Or your family."

As much as she appreciated his words, she knew he couldn't make that guarantee.

SEVEN

Tim reluctantly released Vickie. It was time for them to leave, despite how much he would prefer to continue holding her.

Knowing what he did of her traumatic past and the way she'd been let down by the campus security and the college dean, he didn't blame her for being wary of trusting law enforcement. He could only hope she'd come to trust him.

He opened the bakery's front door so Vickie could exit in front of him. The winter sun glinted in her light-colored hair peeking out beneath her hat, and her cheeks grew rosy from the frosty weather. She was so pretty it made his heart ache.

To distract himself from her charms, he bent to untie Frodo's lead from the metal bike rack outside the bakeshop.

Vickie held out her hand for the dog to sniff. Frodo brushed up against her, lapping up the attention. His partner apparently liked her, too. The dog didn't give approval to many people.

They neared the corner as the traffic light turned red, forcing them to halt. A prickling at the base of Tim's neck sent his senses on alert. He had the distinct impression they were being watched. Slipping his arm around Vickie, he drew her closer as he scanned the area.

"What's wrong?" A tremble punctuated her words.

"I don't know. Maybe nothing."

She gestured with her chin. "Is that Greg?"

Caution tightened the muscle of his shoulders. "Where?"

She looked up at him, her blue-gray eyes troubled. "Across the street."

Tim searched the crowded sidewalk opposite. Sure enough, there was Greg Sherman, the neighborhood security guard, staring at them from the other side of the busy street. His bald head was covered by a dark beanie, and his wide shoulders were squeezed into his security guard uniform jacket. Had he been following them? The man had dodged Tim's calls, and now he was here. An unlikely coincidence.

"Let's go have a chat with old Greg," he said, as soon as the light changed and the Walk sign flashed. He steered both Vickie and Frodo onto the crosswalk.

Greg spun on the balls of his booted feet and darted down the nearest side street. Tim wanted to give pursuit, but with Vickie in tow that wasn't a possibility. Why was Greg following them? But more importantly, why had he run away?

Vickie was surprised to realize the six-story brick structure in the heart of downtown looked like any other office building. There were no markings to indicate this was where the FBI Tactical K-9 Unit had its headquarters. She was even more stunned when Tim took her to a large training center taking up the ground floor. He handed Frodo off to a trainer, who led the German shepherd away.

"How many dogs are used by your unit?" she asked.

"There are eight working dogs and seven puppies of various ages training to become working dogs." An emotion Vickie couldn't quite decipher passed across his face. "Last spring one of our agents went missing. We thought he'd been kidnapped but—" He broke off, his jaw tensing.

Vickie's heart lurched. Something bad had obviously happened to his fellow agent to cause Tim to be so upset. She laid a hand on his arm. "I'm sorry."

His eyes were grim when he met her gaze. "He turned bad. Started working for a crime syndicate. But we didn't know that at first, so in honor of Jake—his name was Jake Morrow—the other agents started collecting puppies to train so we could build up the existing FBI K-9 program."

She swallowed past the lump in her throat. "You used the past tense. Did something happen to Jake?"

He nodded. "Jake was killed. In the end, he did the right thing and protected his own son from being murdered, by sacrificing his own life."

Her stomach dropped. "That's so sad and horrifying. I'm sorry for you and your team's loss."

He covered her hand with his, making her realize she still held on to him. Though she probably should release her grasp, she didn't want to let go. He anchored her, gave her a lifeline in the storm that had overtaken her world.

"Thank you. It hurt. All of us," he said. "But life goes on. And I have to trust that somehow this is all a part of God's plan."

Her heart ached for him and his fellow agents. "I will pray God will heal the wound left by Jake Morrow's choices." Just as she prayed every night that God would heal her own wounds from Ken's assault and the authorities not believing her.

"I'd appreciate that." Tim placed his hand to the small of Vickie's back. "We should get upstairs."

Awareness spread through her and settled in her cheeks. She hoped no one noticed her blush.

Tim led her to the second floor, past cubicles to a conference room that also served as the kitchen area. At the conference table sat a man with salt-and-pepper hair. He wore jeans and a button-down shirt with no tie. He held an electronic tablet, which he set aside with a smile. "Hello." He rose and held out his hand. "I'm Brian Ames."

He had kind eyes, she decided as she shook his hand. "Vickie Petrov."

Brian gestured to the chair beside him. "Have a seat, and we can get started."

Flutters of tensions pranced like little reindeer feet along her nerves as she sat. She linked her fingers together to keep them from shaking. She looked at Tim, desperate to hold on to his promise that he'd protect her and her family.

He put his hand on her shoulder. "It will be all right. I've already given Brian my description of the man who attacked you. He'll combine our details."

She hoped this worked. She stared at her hands and willed her heart to slow down. *Please, Lord, help me to remember.*

"Agent Ramsey, it would be better if you left us," Brian said. "Miss Petrov doesn't need any distractions."

Startled by the man's proclamation, Vickie looked anxiously at Tim.

Tim's eyebrows hitched up. "Right. I'll be back when you're done." He stepped out of the conference room and shut the door behind him.

She gave Brian a weak smile. "I really didn't get more than a fleeting glimpse of the man who attacked me."

"Sometimes that is enough," he assured her, and picked up the stylus for the notebook. "I understand you were attacked twice."

"Yes." She hated the helpless sensation crawling through her.

"Do you think it was the same man both times?"

There was no reason to think it wasn't, was there? "I believe so."

Brian nodded. "What I'm doing is building a composite sketch. At first all I want is for you to tell me your impressions of the attacker. Big boned. Wiry. That sort of thing. Then we'll start working on the face and build on the details Agent Ramsey has already given me."

Her mouth turned to cotton with the weight of responsibility pressing down on her shoulders. It was up to her to help Tim capture the villain. She could only do this with God's help.

"He was big. Bulky. Taller than me." She closed her eyes. "He was just a black blob. He wore a hoodie covering his head and a ski mask." Her eyes flew open. "He had a beard. The night of the fire, I'm sure I saw hair or at least heavy stubble." She shook her head as doubts infiltrated her mind. "I think. Or it could have just been shadows."

"We can start there." Using the stylus, he went to work on the computer. "Walk me through the night of the fire."

Closing her eyes, she prepared herself to relive the assault. But her mind didn't want to cooperate. Instead of recalling the Christmas Eve attacker, her brain took her back to her dorm room three years ago. Ken slamming her against the wall, his groping hands. His stale breath and wild eyes.

Vickie banished the past and tried to concentrate on the present. With her breath expanding in her lungs, she did as Brian asked, recounting the shelter fire, going through each moment as best she could.

Her brain grew tired as the artist showed her dozens of different facial aspects on the tablet, expecting her to pick the closest match to the man she'd seen. But the more images she looked at, the more muddled her memory became as she saw Ken in each feature.

Forty minutes later, Brian tilted his electronic tablet toward her. "What do you think?"

She blinked at the image. There were no eyes or nose, only full lips surrounded by a shadowed jaw beneath a hoodie.

Her heart sank. How would they find the fiend now?

The vague image the forensic artist held up made Tim's stomach drop with disappointment. Apparently Vickie really hadn't seen her attacker's face clearly enough to give more than the barest details of a round head with smooth cheeks tucked inside a dark hoodie. Even adding in his description of the masked attacker hadn't yielded the desired result.

"I'm sorry." Her voice trembled.

Stuffing his frustration into a dark corner, Tim held out his hand. "It's okay. You did great. We'll find him anyway."

She hesitated before slipping her hand into his.

Her slender fingers wrapped around his and held on tight as they walked down the hall to his boss's office. It shouldn't feel so right to have her so close. It shouldn't feel so gratifying.

Special Agent Max West rose as they entered his office, and came around the desk to greet them. Tall and formidable looking, Max was fair and brave and willing to put his own life on the line for his team. Tim couldn't have asked for a better boss. Max had recently become engaged to a nice woman he'd met while working the case to find Jake Morrow.

Max wasn't the only one who'd survived the ordeal and come through to the other side with love. It seemed the whole team had found someone to give their heart to.

Not Tim. He would be the lone holdout no matter what. But with Vickie's palm pressed against his, he was having trouble remembering why he wanted no part of love.

Whoa! Love?

No.

Affection, yes. He held a good amount of affection for the lovely lady at his side. That was a long way from the *L* word.

Vickie's raised eyebrows brought Tim's head out of the clouds. "Max, this is Vickie Petrov," he stated.

"Miss Petrov, Tim has spoken highly of you."

Max hitched a hip on the edge of his desk. "We all appreciate your family's bakery."

A pleased glow lit her eyes. "Thank you, sir. We appreciate your business."

Max shifted his gaze to Tim. "Success?"

"Unfortunately, it was too dark for Vickie to see her attacker's face the night of the shelter fire. He wore a ski mask during yesterday's attack. And we're having trouble tracking down the car that tried to run us over. The plates had been removed," Tim explained.

"I wish I could have been more helpful," Vickie stated with remorse.

Max held up a hand. "Do not feel bad about this. And please, trust that we will do everything in our power to keep you and your family safe."

Vickie glanced at Tim. "I'm learning to."

Tim stood taller and widened his stance. He usually didn't need to have his ego stroked, but hearing her words was satisfying and thrilling.

They said goodbye to Max. On their way out of the building, they ran into fellow agent Nina Atkins. She wore khakis and a dark, long-sleeved T-shirt with the FBI Tactical Team logo on the pocket, and her blond hair peeked out from beneath a knit cap. Beside her stood her partner, a large rottweiler named Sam.

"Nina, this is Vickie Petrov. Vickie, this is Agent Nina Atkins."

"Hi, Nina," Vickie said. "You've been into the bakery."

Nina's brown eyes sparkled. "I thought I recognized you. Is everything okay?"

"Working on it," Tim said.

"Let me know if I can help." Nina waved and took Sam outside.

Tim decided to have Frodo remain in his kennel. He didn't want to have to leave the dog out in the cold while he and Vickie were inside the bakery. Instead of walking back, they took his SUV.

When they entered the bakery the bell over the door announced their arrival. Warmth wrapped around Tim, along with the scents of fresh baking bread and sweets. His stomach rumbled, reminding him it was lunchtime.

"I'll fix you a sandwich," Vickie murmured as she passed him.

He barked a laugh. This assignment definitely had its perks.

As she passed her mother, who was waiting on a steady stream of noontime customers, Vickie paused long enough to drop a kiss on her cheek. The quick greeting gave him an unexpected bump of his heart. They really were a tight-knit family. He automatically reached down to pet Frodo, belatedly remembering he'd left him at the training center.

He followed Vickie to the back of the bakery, where the real artistry happened. He'd never been on this side of the counter and he took in the racks of baked goods, and long counter spaces where Sasha was rolling out dough. Two college-age young men worked nearby, one manning the large oven and the other washing dishes.

Vickie donned protective gloves and set about making two ham and cheese sandwiches on thick slices of crusty bread.

"Can I help?" he asked.

"No, you may not," she replied. "In fact, you shouldn't be back here. Why don't you grab a table and I'll bring them out?"

Nodding, he made his way to the front part of the eatery. He spied an empty table just as Greg, the security guard, walked through the front door. Their gazes collided. For a second, Tim was sure Greg was going to bolt again, but the man squared his shoulders and lumbered forward as if to get in line to order food.

Tim blocked his path. "Why were you following us this morning?"

Greg narrowed his gaze. "Vickie is a friend. I'm worried about her."

"Then why did you run off when we approached you?" Tim wasn't buying his claim of worry.

"I received a call." The man's voice took on a defensive tone. "I had to go do my job."

"I'll verify that," he warned.

Greg frowned. "Go ahead. I've nothing to hide."

"Good. Then you won't mind going to the police station to answer some formal questions," Tim challenged.

"Why? I haven't done anything wrong," the security guard said. "What kind of questions?"

Before Tim could respond, a shrill alarm sounded, bouncing off the bakery walls. Smoke billowed out of the kitchen area. His heart jack-knifed in his chest. He had to save Vickie!

"Everyone out," Tim yelled, as he ran for the kitchen. He paused to grab Irena by the shoulders to prevent her from heading for her husband and daughter. "Out the front."

"But Sasha! Vickie—"

Greg took her hand and helped to usher the crowd out the front door.

Tim grabbed a dish towel from the counter and placed it over his nose and mouth as he ran into the smoke.

EIGHT

Eyes watering from the billowing smoke and flames crawling up the back door of the bakery, Vickie grabbed the fire extinguisher and sprayed white foam at the terrifying wall of fire.

The sharp sound of a fire truck siren penetrated the blaring of the smoke alarm attached to the ceiling. No doubt Tim or her mom had called 911.

Her dad beat at the flames with a wet towel. The two employees had raced toward the front of the store the second they'd realized they were danger to help make sure all the patrons exited safely.

"Dad!" she yelled, unsuccessfully trying to be heard over the cacophony. She wanted to grab him and push him to safety, but the fire extinguisher required both hands. Using her shoulder, she butted him aside. "Go!"

He put his big hands on her shoulders and dragged her with him toward the front of the shop. Then Tim was there with a cloth wrapped around his face so that only his eyes were visible. He took the extinguisher from her and pointed for her and her father to leave.

No way. If it wasn't safe for her, then it wasn't safe for him. Heart pumping with adrenaline, she snagged his elbow and tugged him with her. They made it out to the street as the fire engine rolled past and turned down the alley to the back of the bakery.

Drawing in cleansing breaths of cold air, she searched the crowd for her mom. Vickie sighed with relief to see her parents embracing, safe and unharmed, as were their employees.

"Come on." Tim clasped Vickie's hand. They ran down the alley. The engine roared to a stop as men and women in turnout gear jumped out. Tim drew Vickie to the opposite side of the narrow passage, several feet from the fire.

"Stay here," he instructed, before hustling forward to talk to the fire chief.

This was the arsonist's work. The man had warned her to stop talking to the police. He'd done this as a kind of punishment. Another message. A way of letting her know he could make good on his claim that he could get to her. To the people she loved.

"Vickie!"

She turned to see her parents hurrying toward her. Each had a blanket from the fire department covering their shoulders. When they reached her, her father engulfed her in a hug, while her mother secured a blanket around her.

Irena touched her cheek. "I was so worried."

"I'm fine, Mom." She stepped back to look at them. "Tim got us out safely." He'd risked his own skin for her and her family. She'd be forever grateful. The man was proving she could trust him in ways she'd never thought possible.

"Where *is* Agent Ramsey?" her father asked. "I need to talk to him."

"He's speaking with the fire chief." She gestured to where the two stood near the fire engine. As if he sensed her attention on him, Tim met her gaze. She waved for him to come join her and her parents. He held up one finger, indicating to wait a moment.

A firefighter in turnout gear rounded the back end of the truck and strode over to Vickie and her parents. She couldn't make out his features behind the Plexiglas mask and aspirator covering his face. "It's not safe for you to be here." He pointed toward the opening of the alley, where police were setting up a barricade. "You need to move to the street."

Vickie tucked in her chin. There was something familiar about the firefighter's voice but she couldn't be sure because of the respirator muffling his words. She didn't like the brusque way he delivered the command and the accompanying hand gesture, as if he were shooing them away like pesky insects.

"We will, sir. Thank you," Sasha said, taking Vickie and her mother by the elbow. "We'll wait for Agent Ramsey on the sidewalk."

A few minutes later Tim joined them. "They have the fire under control."

"Agent Ramsey," Sasha said. "You need to speak to Colin. He may have seen something."

At Tim's confused look, Vickie interjected, "He's one of our employees."

"Okay. Right. One of the two young men I saw earlier. Where is he?"

Sasha beckoned to Colin and Ryan, the college freshmen who helped in the back of the shop, and they hustled over.

"Hey, boss," Colin said. "Wow, that was wild."

"This is Agent Ramsey of the FBI. Tell him what you saw this morning," Sasha instructed.

The young man wrinkled his nose. "I don't want to get anyone in trouble."

Tim stepped forward. "If you saw something that might help us, I need to know."

"That security guard who hangs around the bakery a lot was in the alley talking with Mr. Johnson about an hour before the fire broke out," Colin said.

Vickie felt her stomach drop. Not only had Greg shown interest in her and she'd rebuffed him, but Mr. Johnson would profit on an insurance claim if the building were damaged. She shared a glance with Tim. An hour before the fire—that was while she was sitting with the forensic artist at the FBI headquarters. Was Greg really the arsonist? Was he working on behalf of Mr. Johnson?

"Thank you," Tim said. "I'll talk to both men." He looked at them all. "Who called 911?"

Both Colin and Ryan shook their heads. Vickie's parents looked at each other, then back to Tim. "Neither of us."

"We've got class soon," Ryan said. "Can we leave? I want to go home and get cleaned up."

Tim shook his head. "Not yet. I will need my partner to release you. He'll be here any minute."

Vickie assumed the trainer was bringing Frodo over. But surely Tim didn't suspect Colin or Ryan of setting the fire.

"Too bad about the bakery," Ryan said. "I liked working for you."

Sasha ran a hand through his graying hair. "I don't know when you'll be able to come back to work. I'll give you good recommendations," he assured them both.

"Thank you," Colin said. "We'll wait across the street. The bank lobby is warm."

Once the two young men were out of earshot, Vickie said to Tim, "I can assure you those boys didn't set the fire."

"How? How can *you* be as sure as Frodo's ability to smell traces of accelerant, even after a suspect thinks he or she has washed it off?"

Point taken. "I can't, obviously, but I know those guys have no reason to hurt us, or anyone. They have no malice in their hearts. None whatsoever. They've worked for us part-time through high school. We know their families."

Tim reached out and gently gathered her hands

in his, a move so unexpected she didn't have a chance to step back. "Vickie, starting fires isn't always about malice. Sometimes, it's about sickness. Sometimes, good old-fashioned greed. Sometimes, we don't get to know the why, we simply count ourselves lucky to figure out who in a case like this, because that means we can stop it from happening again. I sleep better then."

"Well, I hope you have something to read tonight, Agent, because when Frodo gets here, he's going to clear those boys with two sniffs and a wag." She scanned the crowd. "Greg, on the other hand… I hate to think Greg and Mr. Johnson set fire to the bakery. And the homeless shelter." Had Greg been the one to attack her in the park, too?

"We have no proof it was either of them, but it's worth pursuing," Tim told her.

"But why would Mr. Johnson want to burn down his own buildings?" Irena asked. "And Greg has been so nice to us. We've known the Shermans since the kids were young."

Tim's expression turned grim. "Only Mr. Johnson can answer for sure, but I intend to find out. As for Greg, his feelings for Vickie may be clouding his judgment."

Irena put her arm around Vickie. "Well, I'll talk to his mama."

"Please don't," Tim said quickly. "I don't want to spook Greg. Nor do I want to accuse him of something without proof."

Irena nodded, though Vickie could tell her mother wasn't happy about the situation.

"Mr. Johnson has been on a rampage," Sasha said. "This past summer, when our lease was up, he didn't want to sign another. Instead, he wanted us to rent the building on a month-to-month basis."

Vickie sucked in a quick breath. "Why would he want that?"

"Did you agree to his terms?" Tim asked at the same time.

Her dad nodded. "We had no choice. I wasn't prepared to move. And as to why, I can only guess going month to month allowed him to raise the rent whenever he pleased. Which he has done twice now."

"How can he get away with such a thing?" Vickie asked.

"On a month to month, the law only requires he give a fifteen-day notice before increasing the rent," her father explained. "We've been looking at other locations, but haven't found the right place yet. Looks like we'll need to increase our effort." He turned a sorrowful gaze on the burned-out bakery and Vickie's heart wept for her father.

"I didn't know you were considering moving the bakery." Distress darkened her tone. She shouldn't be surprised they hadn't confided in her. A small voice in her heart whispered that she had done her fair share of keeping secrets from her parents, too.

Her mother placed a hand on her arm. "We didn't want you to worry."

There was a lot of that sentiment going around. Vicki clasped her mom's hand. "I'll help you search for the right place."

"Thank you, dear," Irena said, and pulled her close for a hug.

When she released her, Tim touched Vickie's elbow. "After Frodo and I investigate the scene and the fire chief gives the all clear, you can go inside and gather as much as you can salvage," he said. He looked toward the street. "Frodo's here."

"Thank you, Tim," Vickie said, before he could walk away. "I don't know what we would have done without you."

He seemed to peer through her. "My job is to keep you and your family safe."

He went to talk to one of the police officers. The cop nodded and headed in their direction as Tim took off for his accelerant-detecting dog.

Tim took Frodo's lead from the unit's trainer. "Thanks for driving him over. I didn't want to leave the scene."

"No problem," Faith Rand said, and hurried back to her vehicle.

Frodo lifted his nose to the air.

"Yep, another fire, buddy," Tim said. He grabbed his crime scene kit from his own vehicle. "Okay, boy, let's go to work. I need you to clear a couple of people." He led the dog to the lobby of the bank across the street from the Petrov Bakery, where Colin and Ryan and several other people watched from behind the windows in the heated building.

Tim had Frodo sniff the young men, and when the dog didn't alert, he told them they could leave the scene. Sasha would have their contact information if Tim needed to talk to them again.

When Tim and Frodo reached the sidewalk where the Petrovs stood, the fire chief was already there talking to the family. He clapped Tim on the back. "The scene is yours. I was just telling the Petrovs they could enter through the front door and collect what they can once you're done with your investigation."

"Perfect." Tim turned to Vickie. "I'll text you as soon as Frodo and I have completed our examination of the area."

She frowned. "But the fire started outside. Why can't we go in now?"

"I don't want to confuse Frodo," Tim told her.

He led the German shepherd down the back alley. "Seek," Tim said. Frodo put his nose to the ground and moved steadily closer to the back door of the bakery.

It didn't take long for the dog to find the point of origin. Or the evidence that linked the fire to the other cases of arson: matches, remnants of cotton fibers and the remains of a cigarette.

Feeding Frodo kibble from the pouch at his

waist, Tim said a thankful prayer that the arsonist hadn't used paraffin wax as he had on the shelter fire. This burn was a warning for Vickie, making good on his threat, hoping to silence her about what she had witnessed the night of the homeless shelter fire.

Anger burned in Tim's gut. The maniac responsible for terrorizing Vickie would pay for his crimes.

Tim thought through possible scenarios. Was Johnson paying Greg to set the fires? Did Johnson hope to collect the insurance money? Or was Greg setting the fires for his own purposes?

NINE

After helping the Petrovs pack up what they could carry from the bakery, Tim had two police officers escort them home. He wasn't taking any chances. He and Frodo returned to headquarters and went upstairs to Dylan O'Leary's computer cave. The team's tech expert was at his station when they entered.

"Hey, do you have a moment?" Tim asked.

Dylan lifted his hands from the keyboard and spun in his chair to face him. "Of course, bro. What's up?"

Tim smiled at the moniker. Dylan was the closest Tim had ever come to having a brother. They'd been roommates until Dylan had married this past fall. "I need you to do a deep background check on two people." He gave him Barry Johnson's and Greg Sherman's names.

"I need to know financials, criminal history and anything else you can dig up that might be relevant to my arson cases." He supplied him with the dates and properties.

"Sure thing," Dylan said, already turning to his computer.

"Do you mind if I wait?" Tim asked.

"Not at all." His friend opened a drawer. "There's treats here."

"Thanks." Tim grabbed a handful and for the

next few minutes put Frodo through a set of exercises. It was best to have the dog work for his food as often as possible, to keep his mind and body active when not out in the field.

When he'd run out of treats, Tim instructed Frodo to a down position, then waited to see what Dylan dredged up on his suspects.

An hour later, the tech expert said, "Greg Sherman has a criminal history. Petty theft five years ago."

"No arson?"

"Nope. And no big deposits in his bank accounts."

Johnson could be paying Greg in cash. "And Mr. Johnson?"

"Barry Johnson has no criminal history. However, he is financially strapped."

"But he owns several properties downtown."

"He does indeed. And all the burned properties belong to him. He's drowning in expenses."

Tim rubbed his chin. "Reason enough to burn down the buildings and commit insurance fraud."

"Can you prove it?" Dylan asked.

"Not yet," Tim said. "But I will."

"Let me know if there is anything else I can do," his buddy told him.

Tim hesitated as some force within brought to mind the man who'd assaulted Vickie in college. "There is something. I want you to find out all you can on a guy named Ken Leland. I want to know where he is and what he's doing."

"Who's this?"

Wanting to respect her privacy, Tim hedged, "A man from Vickie Petrov's past. They attended college together." He gave Dylan the name of the school.

His colleague tilted his head. "Are we using government resources for a personal matter?"

"No, of course not." Tim didn't miss the amusement in his friend's eyes. "It's not like that."

Dylan grinned. "It sure looks like *that* to me. You've got it bad. Not that I blame you. Vickie Petrov is a pretty lady. And nice."

Tim shook his head. "You don't know what you're talking about. I'm protecting Vickie. Nothing more. There's nothing else going on."

"Bro, you can deny your feelings all you want, but it's written all over your face."

Tim's stomach churned. Was he in denial about his feelings for Vickie? "So I care about her. There's no crime in that."

Dylan grew serious. "No. But don't lead her on. I know you, bro. You're a die-hard bachelor."

"I am," Tim confirmed, only the conviction didn't resonate through him as it normally did.

"Be careful. Don't hurt her."

"That's the last thing I want to do." Tim's mouth went dry as his friend's words ricocheted through his brain. He needed to get his head on straight and remember Vickie was a victim of a crime and it was his job to bring the criminal to justice, not to fall for the woman he was protecting.

With resolve to keep his emotions in check, Tim headed for the door. "Come on, Frodo. Time we have a chat with Mr. Johnson."

"Have a seat, Mr. Johnson." Tim held on to his patience as he instructed the older man with a gesture toward the metal chair pushed up to a matching table in the center of the Billings Police Department's interrogation room. Police Chief Fielding stepped in behind them and closed the door.

The sheen of sweat on Mr. Johnson's brow glistened in the intense glare of the overhead fluorescent lights. His expensive wing tip shoes scuffed along the linoleum floor as he scooted past Frodo with a look of distaste. The dog sniffed the man's shoes and pant leg and then lifted his nose toward his hands. Johnson recoiled, clearly afraid the dog would bite.

After a moment, the German shepherd lost interest in him and lay down near the door.

"I demand to know why you've brought me here," Mr. Johnson said as he plopped his rotund self on the metal chair.

The chief gave a slight nod, indicating for Tim to take the lead and question the suspect.

Tim laid out four file folders. "I'd like to know

why several of your buildings have been targeted by an arsonist. And why you didn't mention your other properties the night of the shelter fire."

Mr. Johnson took a handkerchief from the breast pocket of his wool coat and mopped his forehead. Stressed by guilt? "I didn't realize these incidents were connected."

Tim arched an eyebrow. "Don't play me for dumb. I've already checked with your insurance company and you've filed three claims." He opened the first file, which showed the burned-out shell of a three-bedroom, two-bath house on a residential street. "The house on Lazy Willow Lane." Tim opened another file, revealing the charred remains of the back half of a building. "The tire store downtown." He tapped the third file without opening it. Mr. Johnson couldn't deny having seen the damage to the shelter. "The homeless shelter."

The man made a face and looked away from the files. "Someone is out to get me."

Tim didn't buy the rationalization for a second. The property owner stood to gain from the blazes in insurance payouts. "Now Petrov Bakery."

Tim slammed his palm on the table, eliciting a startled yelp from Johnson. Frodo rose to all fours and growled. Tim gave him the stay command with his other hand. "And I'm sure I'll find a way to connect you to the house on Picador Way."

Visibly gathering his composure, Johnson held

up a hand. "Now wait a minute." He patted his chest. "You don't think I'm responsible for these fires, do you?" His gaze darted to the police chief. "Why would I want to burn down my own buildings?"

Tim opened the last file folder and turned it so that Mr. Johnson could view the contents. "Your financials. You're in the red by millions. Setting a fire and claiming the insurance money is one of the oldest and most common money scams out there."

Clearly shaken, Johnson shook his head emphatically. "No. I did not set these fires."

Prepared for the denial, Tim said, "I've also talked to your current tenants in your other holdings. It seems you've been very reluctant to renew leases over the past year, demanding they go month to month. And you've increased the rent on all of your tenants. Some have even suggested you wanted them to vacate. Which begs the question, why?"

"I don't have to explain myself to you," Johnson said. "You can't pin these fires on me. You have no proof that I was involved."

"Why did you try to run Vickie Petrov down?" Tim asked the pointed question, hoping to trip him up.

Johnson reared back. "Excuse me? What are you talking about?"

"What were you doing behind Petrov Bakery this morning prior to the fire?"

"I was checking the electrical meter," Johnson said.

Tim made eye contact with Chief Fielding. Okay, then. They were halfway to a confession. Johnson's admission placed him at the scene of the crime.

"The electric company claims the building is draining too much power and is leveling me with fines," Johnson continued. "I'm sure it's the Petrovs who are causing the problem, though I can't prove it. No one else in the building uses much energy."

"Why not talk directly to Sasha Petrov, rather than skulking around the back of the building?"

"I wasn't skulking. I've been keeping tabs on the usage."

"Why was Greg Sherman with you?"

"He's my employee," Johnson said. "I've tasked him with keeping an eye on the meter. If you don't believe me, ask him. Check with the electric company."

"I will," Tim replied. "How much are you paying Greg to set these fires?"

Johnson sputtered. "I am not paying him to set the fires."

"Why would someone target buildings you own?"

Spreading his hands wide, Johnson said, "I don't know."

Tim hammered at him. "Why are you trying to push your tenants out?"

Johnson frowned, but clamped his lips together, clearly unwilling to divulge his motivations.

"Did you send someone to assault Vickie?"

Johnson's eyes widened with shock. "I would never." His gaze narrowed. "You need to talk to Greg. He's got a thing for the Petrov girl. She's trouble. That whole family is trouble."

Anger ignited within Tim's chest. "Enough trouble for you to want them gone?"

Johnson's expression turned bulldoggish. "If you're going continue questioning me, I want my lawyer present. Otherwise I want to leave. I have rights."

Frustrated by the lack of progress in eliciting a confession from Johnson, Tim met Chief Fielding's gaze. The older man shrugged and gestured toward the door.

Tim gathered the files. "Sit tight," he said to Johnson. With Frodo at his heels, he followed Chief Fielding into the hall.

"We don't have enough to hold him," Fielding said. "The insurance companies will be doing their own investigations, and if the FBI wants to make a case against the man, you're going to need to come up with more than you have."

"I know," Tim muttered. "I'm counting on Greg Sherman to provide some answers. Because right now all I have are more questions."

If Barry Johnson really wasn't involved, who was burning down his properties? And why? Was Greg trying to hurt Vickie?

"I'm releasing Johnson," Chief Fielding said. "But I'll warn him not to leave town."

Tim nodded. He didn't like letting the man off the hook, especially without answers.

His phone dinged just then, indicating a text coming in. It was from Dylan.

Tim read: I have the info you asked for.

"I'm heading back to my office," he said to the chief. "Let me know when your officers bring Greg in."

"Will do." Fielding reentered the interrogation room.

Tim and Frodo left the police station and headed to the FBI building a few blocks away. Tim found Dylan in his office. "You found something on Ken Leland?"

"I did." Dylan took off his black-framed glasses and rubbed the lens with a cloth. "Leland didn't graduate from college. He left in the middle of his last semester under mysterious circumstances."

Interesting. Tim leaned against the desk. "Mysterious how?"

Putting his glasses back on, Dylan made a face. "The school is all hush-hush about it. They won't release his records without a warrant."

Since this inquiry into Ken wasn't part of an

official investigation, a warrant wouldn't be easy to obtain. "Where is he now?"

"Here's the thing," Dylan said. "Ken Leland disappeared."

Tim was surprised even as a sense of disquiet sneaked beneath the collar of his shirt and tightened the muscles of his shoulders. Agitation churned in his gut. "What do you mean, disappeared?"

Dylan shrugged. "I couldn't find any record of Ken Leland after he left college."

"How could that happen?"

A smirk settled over Dylan's face. "He changed his name. He was clever about it, but not clever enough." Dylan tapped his keyboard and brought up a photo of a dark-haired man with dark eyes. His unsmiling mouth was a flat slash emphasizing a square jaw. "He's going by his mother's maiden name, Benson. Who just happens to be Barry Johnson's wife's sister."

His mind reeling from the news, Tim said, "Let me get this straight. Ken Leland, aka Ken Benson, is Barry Johnson's nephew." A niggling at the back of his mind clamored for attention.

"Yep. And here's where it gets even more interesting." Dylan zoomed out from the photo of Ken to reveal it to be on a driver's license. "Benson dropped his first name and is using his middle name."

"Joseph," Tim stated, staring at the screen. A memory of Mr. Johnson claiming to have a nephew working as a Billings firefighter surfaced and scorched through his brain like a flash of lightning. "He's with BFD."

"How did you know?" Dylan gave a mock pout. "That was my grand finale statement." He clicked a few more keys and another photo appeared, of a man in turnout gear holding his helmet at his side. There was no mistaking Ken Leland, aka Joseph Benson.

Tim had a bad feeling in the pit of his stomach. He felt like he was staring at a jigsaw puzzle. How did the pieces connect? The man who'd assaulted Vickie in college now resided in Billings. And he was a firefighter and nephew to Barry Johnson, landlord to the Petrovs. Coincidence? Unlikely. But to what end?

How did Greg fit in? Who was the arsonist? Had it been Ken or Greg who attacked Vickie in the park?

"We need to bring this guy in for questioning," Tim said. "I'll start the paperwork for a warrant, as well."

"You think he's involved in your case?"

"I don't know what to think."

Tim's cell phone rang. He answered. The man on the other side said, "Sir, this is Officer Wainwright with Billings PD. Chief Fielding asked me to contact you. We've been unable to locate Greg Sherman. He's not at his place of residence."

Tim's stomach dropped. Had Greg skipped town?

"The chief has put out a BOLO on the man," Wainwright continued. "If he's running, we'll catch him."

"I have another suspect I need brought in." Tim gave the officer Joseph Benson's name and the information that he worked for the fire department.

"I'll tell the chief," the officer said, before hanging up.

Tim hoped the "be on the lookout" would net the security guard and Joseph, aka Ken.

"Greg Sherman is missing," he told Dylan.

Tim wanted, needed, to be with Vickie and her family. It wasn't that he didn't trust the Billings police officers stationed in front of her house to keep her safe. His need came from his heart, he realized in a moment of clarity.

A place he'd never thought he'd open again.

But somehow Vickie had infiltrated his defenses. His feelings for her went beyond caring and affection. Despite his resolve not to let himself fall for her, he had. He loved Vickie.

He wasn't sure what that would mean in the future or even if there was a future for them. For now, he had to see her, be with her. He needed to assure himself she was unharmed.

He called the Petrovs' home. The phone just

rang. Fear clutched at him, balling his insides into knots. He dialed Vickie's cell and it went directly to voice mail, as if the device had been turned off. Alarm spiraled through his brain and revved up his blood pressure.

"I'm heading to Vickie Petrov's home," he told Dylan.

"Ah."

There was a world of meaning behind the two-letter word, but Tim chose to ignore it. He didn't have time for another lecture.

Gripping Frodo's lead, Tim raced out of the building. A prayer lifted from his lips. "Please, dear God, don't let anything be wrong. Let me be panicking for nothing."

TEN

Vickie stood in the kitchen with confusion and frustration warring within her. She'd left her cell phone on the counter to charge, as she always did when she was home, and now it was gone. Had her mom or dad used it? Why? They had their own cells and the landline if they needed to make a call.

She stepped into the living room, where her parents sat on the couch watching a movie. "Have either of you seen my cell phone?"

Dad picked up the remote and paused the screen. "Is it charging on the counter?"

"It's not there," she replied.

"Could you have taken it upstairs with you earlier?" her mother asked.

"I didn't." At least she didn't remember doing so, but when she'd returned home from working with the forensic artist, she'd been a bit scattered.

Maybe she'd only thought to set it to charging, but had forgotten on her way to her room for a much needed nap. Not that she'd slept. Her thoughts had been in constant motion. Still were… The past and the present kept jumbling together until she wasn't sure which way was up.

Her feelings for Tim clouded her mind and confused her heart. She could have easily taken her cell phone to her room.

"I'll go check upstairs." She hurried to her bedroom, and sure enough, her phone was in her purse.

The sound of the doorbell chime jolted her pulse. Tim? They weren't expecting him, but a flood of anticipation had her hurrying down the stairs. "I'll get it!"

She yanked open the door and stumbled back a step as her gaze collided with Greg Sherman's.

Vickie's heart slammed against her rib cage. Greg Sherman stood on the porch. He didn't have on his security guard uniform. Instead he wore jeans, work boots and a leather jacket. In his arms he held a large picnic basket and a bouquet of flowers.

She looked over his shoulder toward the police cruiser parked across the street. Why had the officers in the vehicle allowed Greg to knock on her door? Had Tim already questioned Greg and released him?

Her father joined her at the doorway, while her mother hovered behind them. Sasha folded his arms over his chest and stared hard at Greg. "What are you doing here?"

"Hello, Mr. Petrov," he said. "Pastor John asked me to bring this basket over." He adjusted it in his arms. "My mom and some of the church ladies got together and made your family a care package."

Irena squeezed in between Vickie and Sasha.

"That's so sweet," she cooed. "Why don't you come in?"

Vickie wasn't sure about allowing Greg inside. "Mom," she warned beneath her breath.

Waving away her worry, her mom reached for the basket. "Here, let me take that."

"I'll get it." Her dad clasped the edges of the basket. Her mother opened the lid, revealing two casserole dishes covered with foil, a tossed green salad and a bottle of her mom's favorite sparkling apple cider. Seemed Greg was telling the truth about the food.

"I know my mom's broccoli and cheddar cheese casserole won't be nearly as good as something you would make at the bakery, but it's my favorite." He stepped inside and held out the bouquet of flowers to Vickie. "These are for you."

Reluctant to accept the offering, she hesitated as she shut the door, but remained in place, ready to yank it open again to call for help. "You didn't have to."

A resigned smile stretched his lips. "I want to apologize for everything you and your family have been through." He lowered his voice. "The cops questioned me about the bakery fire."

Wariness made her tighten her fingers around the door handle. "I knew Agent Ramsey wanted to talk to you."

Greg frowned. "I didn't talk to him. But I told the other cops Mr. Johnson had me meet him behind the bakery." Their visitor made a face. "He wanted me to spy on you. Or rather the building. He says the bakery uses too much energy. But that's not true. I checked all the meters for the whole block and the bakery doesn't take any more power than the other businesses."

"We pay the electric bill," Sasha said. "What does it matter to him how much energy we use?"

Shaking his head, Greg said, "Beats me. He's been acting very strange lately. Which is why I've decided to quit." Greg looked at Vickie. "I'm going to join the military. Find my path in life."

Surprise washed through her. She wondered if Tim knew this. And what he thought of it. "That's a big decision."

Greg nodded. "It is. But I feel good about it. Pastor John has been helping me to see I need to change my environment. He has a friend in the army that he's going to have me talk to about joining. It's time I moved on."

Vickie couldn't say she was saddened by the news. Not having to worry about dodging Greg's attention would be welcome. She had a hard time reconciling this version of him with the thought of him being the arsonist or the man who'd attacked her. Was he a good actor?

"Sasha, take the basket into the kitchen," Irena instructed. To Greg, she said, "Please thank your mother and let her know we appreciate the gesture."

"I will."

An awkward silence descended.

"Let me put these pretty flowers in water." Irena took the bouquet from Vickie with a look that clearly said *be nice.*

Keeping distance between them, Vickie led Greg into the living room, hoping he'd leave.

He moved to look out the front window. "Why are the police outside?"

"After everything that has happened lately, Agent Ramsey thought it would be a good idea to have them watching over us." And she sent up a silent prayer that the officers had already alerted him that Greg was here, and Tim was on his way.

"You like Agent Ramsey," Greg said. "It's pretty obvious."

She blinked back her surprise at his observation. Acceptance seeped into her core. She *did* like Tim, more than liked really, but she certainly wasn't going to discuss her feelings with Greg.

Her gaze fell on the black box still sitting on the mantel. She picked it up and held it out to Greg. "I can't accept this."

He tucked in his chin and made no move to take it. "What is it?"

She frowned and popped open the lid. "The necklace you left on the porch Christmas Eve."

He shook his head. "I didn't leave that. It's pretty, though."

She sucked in a quick breath. Her hand shook

as his words reverberated through her skull. "You didn't give this to me?"

"No." Concern darkened his eyes. "Are you okay? You look like you might pass out or something."

If Greg didn't leave the necklace, then who did? Her pulse ticked faster with anxiety. She needed to talk to Tim.

"I need to make a phone call." Because she'd left her cell phone upstairs in her room, she hurried to her father's study to use the house landline. She picked up the extension and pressed it to her ear. There was no dial tone. Unease slithered down her spine.

She rushed to the kitchen, where her mom was dishing out food as her father poured apple cider into glasses. Greg had taken a seat at the table.

"Dad, the landline isn't working. Can I use your cell?"

He set the glass and the bottle down. "What do you mean, not working?"

"There's no dial tone," she said.

"I'll get my cell phone," he stated. "I left it in the car when we came home."

"Mine's in my purse," her mom said. "It's hanging in the hall closet."

Before Vickie and her father could step out of the kitchen a loud explosion from the attached garage rocked the house. A wall of hazy smoke quickly filled the living room and invaded the kitchen. The house was on fire!

Adrenaline spiked through Vickie. Fear clogged her throat. She had to save her family. "The back door…"

"The house is burning!" her mom cried.

Greg jumped up, knocking over the chair. "We have to get out!"

Sasha wrapped his arms around Irena and hustled her to the rear door.

But when he tried to turn the handle, it wouldn't budge. He worked the locks, but the door still wouldn't open. "It's been nailed shut from the outside!"

Vickie's breath stalled in her lungs. Someone had closed off their escape route.

The smoke grew denser. Vickie choked, her eyes watering from the toxic haze.

Her mother coughed.

Greg covered his mouth and nose with the crook of one arm.

A loud banging at the front door startled them.

"Fire department! Call out!" A firefighter rushed inside wearing turnout gear, a mask covering his face and carrying a pickax. Greg darted past him to safety.

"Hurry!" The fireman waved them toward the door.

Vickie followed her parents, making sure they made it to the front porch. But before she could get out herself, the firefighter snagged an arm around her waist and dragged her backward. He slammed the front door and shoved her away from him. He jammed the pickax beneath the door handle, effectively keeping anyone from entering, and trapping the two of them inside.

Taking shallow breaths that stung her lungs, Vickie tried to make sense of what was happening.

The firefighter advanced toward her.

She backed up until she hit the staircase. "Are you insane? What are you doing? Who are you?"

The man stopped and picked up a small canister from the floor near the garage door. She hadn't noticed it in her panic. The cylinder emitted billowing smoke. The explosion hadn't been from a fire, after all. There were no flames. An elaborate ruse to get her alone. But why?

The man yanked open the door to the garage and tossed the canister inside, then shut it again. Slowly, he turned to face her and removed his helmet and facemask.

Vickie's worst nightmare stared at her.

Ken.

ELEVEN

The world tilted. Vickie hadn't been mixing up the past and the present. He was here, in the flesh. Dressed as a fireman. "I don't understand. How can you be here?"

His gaze narrowed. "Fate."

A chill of terror washed over her. She looked for an escape, but the only place she could go was up the stairs. She took another step back. "Why are you doing this?"

"You ruined my life." The malice in his brown eyes cut through her like a sharp knife. "You have to pay." He lunged at her.

Panic revved her blood. He was going to kill her. Spurred into action by the thought, she fled up the staircase, praying she made it to the safety of the bathroom at the end of the hall, where she could lock him out.

Ken pounded up the steps behind her, his heavy footfalls echoing inside her head like nails being pounded into a coffin.

"Please, Lord, help me!" she cried out.

Her parents would alert the police officers. They would come to her rescue. They would call Tim.

She just had to survive long enough for help to reach her. She didn't want to die. She wanted to live. She wanted to tell Tim...

She reached the bathroom and grabbed the door, putting her weight into shutting it behind her, but Ken was hot on her heels. He outweighed her by at least a hundred pounds and easily pushed the door inward, sending her stumbling backward. With one giant hand, he shoved her to the floor.

She scrambled away from him, but there was nowhere to go. "Stop! You have to stop."

Looming over her like some monster from a horror movie, he said, "I won't stop until you're dead."

"What did I do to you?" He was the one who had assaulted her. He'd taken so much from her. Her dreams. Her sense of self. Her ability to trust.

"You took everything away from me!" He slammed his fist into the wall, leaving a gaping hole.

His words made no sense. How could she reason with him when he was clearly out of his mind?

But she had to try if she wanted to live. *Keep him talking*, she told herself. Give the authorities time to rescue her. "How did I ruin your life?"

"You were a tease," he growled. "You were just like the others. All teases. Letting a guy think you wanted him, only to refuse."

There were others he'd assaulted? She shuddered with dread and revulsion. "I never led you on."

"Yes, you did," he insisted. "And then you went running to the dean."

"Dean Abernathy didn't believe me. No one believed me."

Ken laughed, a horrible sound that bounced off the pale yellow walls. "Of course they didn't. They believed me. But when the others came forward after they heard about what you'd claimed—" He clenched his fists. "Not even my parents' money could make them accept my version of things. They expelled me. I couldn't graduate or get my degree. If it weren't for my uncle, I'd be jobless and homeless."

"But you have a life now," she pointed out, trying to make sense of what he was telling her. Other women had filed complaints against Ken and the dean had had to expel him. She'd cut off all ties to the school so had not heard about this. "You're helping people as a firefighter."

"That's right," he said. "And I'm good at it. But then I saw you. Of all the places to land in the world… I'd forgotten you were from here." His mouth stretched into a thin line. "It was as if Fate had decided to throw me a bone. A bone I intend to bury. It's time for you to die."

He advanced on her.

Terror flooded her system. The words of her self-defense instructor echoed through her head. *If you can't run away, then don't go down without a fight.*

There was no way she would let Ken win.

He'd taken too much from her already. Her gaze snagged on her curling iron at the edge of the counter near her head. She pushed to her feet and grabbed the iron.

"Get out of the way!" Tim shouted to the other cars as he drove through the late afternoon traffic. He had to reach Vickie, to assure himself she and her parents were safe.

With Greg Sherman in the wind and the discovery that Ken Leland was in town, Tim wouldn't take any chances. His heart thumped, urging him to go faster. He hit the switch that turned on the strobe lights attached to the roof of his vehicle.

As Tim brought his SUV to a halt outside the Petrov home, several things hit him at once. Mr. and Mrs. Petrov were running out the front door in a wave of smoke. The door slammed shut behind them. Greg Sherman stood on the lawn, doubled over, gagging and coughing. A police cruiser sat at the curb with two officers sitting inside, not moving.

Alarmed by the scene, Tim jumped from his vehicle, released Frodo from his compartment, then raced to the cruiser. Frodo barked and paced while Tim skidded to a halt, then yanked open the driver's-side door. The officers were unconscious. Or worse, dead.

He reached inside to check the nearest man's

neck and found a pulse. Then he checked the other one. Both alive.

"Agent Ramsey!" Sasha Petrov ran toward him. He coughed as he forced out his words. "Vickie's still inside."

With his heart dropping to his toes, Tim grabbed his cell phone and dialed 911. He handed the device to Sasha. "Get help."

Then Tim, with Frodo at his heels, rushed for the front door. It wouldn't budge. He used his shoulder as a battering ram and still the door held.

"Agent Ramsey," Greg yelled. "There's a fireman in there. He and Vickie are trapped inside."

Not trapped. Ken was extracting some sort of revenge on Vickie.

Gripped by the certain knowledge that he had to act fast, Tim spied a garden gnome peeking out of the snow-covered flowerbed. He heaved it at the window, shattering the pane into thousands of pieces that rained down to litter the snow.

Not wanting Frodo to cut his paws on broken glass, Tim gave the command, "Stay."

Then he climbed through the opening, his pants snagging and ripping on shards of glass clinging to the window frame. Inside the house, a layer of smoke hung in the air, but he saw no flames. He released his sidearm from its holster.

A scream came from upstairs. *Vickie!*

Pushing aside his panic, Tim ran for the staircase and noticed the front door. Anger erupted in his chest at the sight of the pickax wedged beneath the handle. He yanked the offending object away, then opened the door and let out a sharp whistle as he turned and sprinted up the stairs. Frodo raced inside and slipped past him.

A cacophony of noise filled the house. Frodo growling. A man cursing.

Tim reached the landing. Vickie stood in the doorway of the bathroom, holding a curling iron like a baseball bat and swinging at the man dressed as a fireman. He held up his hands in defense while shaking his leg in a useless attempt to dislodge Frodo. The dog's teeth were clenched around his ankle in a bite and hold. Frodo dragged the man toward Tim.

From outside the house, the wail of sirens announced backup had arrived.

"Ken!" Tim shouted, drawing his attention.

The man swiveled toward him, his gaze wild. "Call off your dog!"

"Let Vickie go." Tim met her panicked gaze and motioned with his free hand. "Come to me."

She slid along the wall past Ken, who grabbed at her. "No!"

Vickie dodged Ken's reach. Frodo swung his powerful head back and forth. Off balance, Ken fell to the floor.

Tim tucked Vickie behind him, while keeping his gun aimed at Ken's heart. Then he let out a short whistle. Frodo released his captive and backed up, growling and baring his teeth.

"Hands on your head," Tim shouted. "On your knees."

Ken hesitated, his eyes on Frodo.

"Do it!" Tim commanded. "Or I release him."

Slowly, Ken went to his knees and placed his laced fingers on the back of his head. "All right, already. Call off your dog."

"Ramsey!" Chief Fielding's voice carried up the staircase.

"Up here." Tim waited until several officers rushed up the stairs, followed by the chief.

"Come," Tim instructed Frodo. The dog immediately obeyed, allowing the officers to take Ken into custody and lead him away in handcuffs.

Once they were alone, Vickie shook like a leaf in a windstorm. After holstering his weapon, Tim rubbed her arms. She stared up at him with wide, unfocused eyes. Shock. He drew her to his chest and held her. "You're safe now."

She took a shuddering breath. "I was so scared. I thought I was going to die."

"You held him off with a curling iron." He couldn't keep the pride and awe from his voice.

"It was the only thing within reach," she said. "Not that I could have done much damage against a man in heavy gear. But his head was my target."

"Hey, whatever works. You're alive."

"You saved me." She smiled and looked toward Frodo. "You both did."

"You were doing a great job of fending for yourself." Tim's heart continued to beat at a fast clip. He knew it wasn't just from the adrenaline, but because he still held her in his arms.

"Agent Ramsey, everything okay?" Chief Fielding's voice traveled up the stairs. "We're taking the suspect to the station."

Reluctantly, Tim released his hold on Vickie. "We need to go. You'll have to give a statement. And I want to question Ken Leland."

Keeping a hand to her back, Tim escorted her downstairs and to the porch. Her parents waited by the chief's squad car. Greg Sherman was talking with officers. An ambulance was leaving the scene, most likely taking the two unconscious officers to the hospital. Ken Leland sat in the back of a cruiser as it sped away down the street.

Vickie melted into Tim for a moment. He met her gaze, then glanced up at the ball of mistletoe hanging overhead.

"Tradition." He leaned close, intending to kiss her lips, but at the last second she turned her head. His kiss landed on her soft cheek. Confusion infused him. Why had she turned away?

She stepped out of his reach. "Thank you for everything," she whispered, and then hurried down the stairs to the waiting arms of her family.

As he and Frodo walked to his SUV, Tim wondered when or if he'd see Vickie Petrov again. The thought of not doing so shattered his heart as effectively as the garden gnome had shattered the window.

After leaving the Petrov home, he followed the police cruiser transporting Ken Leland, aka Joseph Benson, to the police station. Vickie would give her statement at the scene. If the investigation required more, she'd go to the station at a later date.

The drive into town gave Tim time to process the kiss. Or rather the nonkiss.

What had he been thinking?

He hadn't been. That was the problem. From the second he'd realized she was in peril, his brain had gone offline and his heart had taken over. The sight of her brandishing that curling iron at Ken was imprinted on Tim's mind. She'd looked achingly beautiful and terrified at the same time.

Pride and admiration filled his chest. She had so much strength and courage. She hadn't wilted beneath the terror of Ken's assault. Tim thanked God he and Frodo had arrived in time, before the situation had turned deadly. The tangible relief continued to pulse through his veins.

And the moment he and Vickie had passed beneath the mistletoe, he'd given in to the overwhelming need to kiss her.

However, she'd made it perfectly clear she

wasn't receptive to his attention when she'd turned away from him.

Don't lead her on, bro. You're a confirmed bachelor.

Dylan's words echoed in his head as he waited for Ken to be brought to the interrogation room. For so many years now, Tim had used the phrase "confirmed bachelor" as a shield against getting involved. But now the words rang hollow.

But it didn't matter. Vickie wasn't interested in him. This was a place he'd been before. He'd survived last time he'd fallen in love and that love hadn't been returned. And he would survive now.

Shoring up his defenses might take him a few days, but he would do it. No need to pine for something that had never really started. Once this case was closed, he'd file away all thoughts of Vickie, too.

"Good job, Tim," Special Agent in Charge Max West said as he joined Tim in the hallway. Beside Max, his partner, a regal looking boxer named Opal, came to a halt.

"Thank you, sir." Doing a good job was important. And what Tim needed to focus on. Not the pretty baker who'd stolen his heart.

Max gestured with his chin toward the closed door of another interrogation room. "Chief Fielding had Johnson brought back in. The guy is seated in there with his lawyer. I've already had a chat with him. He's pinning all the arson on his nephew."

"And what about the assaults on Vickie?" Tim asked.

"Johnson claims ignorance," Max said.

Chief Fielding joined them outside the room.

"Any word on your officers?" Max asked him.

Fielding nodded. "Both men will be fine. Their coffee had been drugged with a sedative. They'd stopped at a diner on the way to the house," the chief told them. "The waitress at the diner places Ken there at the same time."

"Here's our suspect now," Max said, as two officers escorted Ken from booking.

Beside Max his partner, Opal, let out a low growl.

The hair on Frodo's back rose as he bared his teeth.

Ken's turnout gear had been removed and he now wore civilian clothes. His brown eyes stared at Tim with unveiled hatred. Tim and Max, along with the dogs, stepped out of the way as the officers led Ken into the room and forced Ken to sit, and linked his cuffed hands to a chain threaded through a ring in the middle of the table.

Tim and Max stepped in to the small space after the two officers left and took seats across from Ken, while Chief Fielding leaned against a wall. Tim would imagine the three of them made an intimidating picture, yet Ken appeared unfazed.

Not even the presence of the two dogs—Frodo sitting at attention next to Tim, with his dark eyes trained on Leland, and Opal, who sat at Max's side staring just as intently—seemed to bother him.

"We have you solid for assault and attempted murder," Tim said, as evenly as he could, but the anger he felt leached through each word. "You're going to prison for a long time."

Ken held his gaze, his lip curling ever so slightly.

Max spoke. "But you could do yourself a favor by cooperating. Maybe make those years a little less torturous. Tell us about the fires."

"I don't know what you're talking about," Ken spat.

Tim laid out the photos of the five fires they suspected he had ignited. "All of these places belong to your uncle, Barry Johnson." They'd finally found the connection on the other residential property. The deed was in Barry Johnson's wife's name.

Ken flicked a glance at the row of images. He shook his head and leaned back. He moved his arms as if to cross them over his chest, but the chain yanked his arms back to the table.

"Just so you know," Max said. "Your uncle is in another room right now. You think he's going to take the blame for the fires? He's serving you up like fish on a platter."

Tim detected a spark of apprehension in Ken's

gaze. "He's going to walk away from this with money in his pockets, while you rot in jail."

Ken's jawed worked.

"We have officers at your apartment tearing the place apart," Max said. "We'll have all the evidence we need to convict you of five counts of arson on top of the charges of assault and attempted murder. You have few precious seconds to come clean. If we leave this room without hearing your story, your uncle walks a free man while you go directly to jail."

Sweat dripped down the side of Ken's face. He seemed to be internally debating with himself. Finally, he said, "It was all Uncle Barry. If you find anything in my apartment, he put it there to set me up."

It seemed the two relatives were willing to sell each other out. "Why would he want to burn down his own properties?"

Ken snorted. "He's got a gambling addiction. He needs the cash."

"So you did the deeds in exchange for what?" Max asked.

"You can't prove I did anything," Ken retorted. "Even if you find something in my apartment, it's only circumstantial."

"When did you decide to go after Vickie?" Tim interjected. "Was it before or after you set the fire at the homeless shelter?"

Nostrils flaring, Ken stayed silent. Rage seethed in his brown eyes.

"Did your uncle tell you she was there?" Max pressed.

"She saw you and you were afraid she'd ID you," Tim continued. "You decided to silence her. It was your opportunity to make her pay for getting you kicked out of college."

Ken lifted his chin. "I want a lawyer."

Tim's fingers curled. Not even a lawyer could get Ken out of this hot water. "We'll get you your lawyer. But with Vickie's testimony and mine, there's only one way this goes."

Chief Fielding pushed away from the wall. "I'll have the prisoner escorted to his cell while he waits for his attorney."

Tim and Max led the dogs out of the police station. Fresh snow fell as they walked to their respective vehicles.

"Take a week off," Max told Tim. "You deserve it."

"Thanks. I will." Though he had no idea what he and Frodo would do. Maybe fly down to Florida to visit his mother and her family. Frodo didn't mind flying and a little sunshine and time away from Montana and a certain pretty baker might be just the remedy Tim needed.

TWELVE

Scrubbing the display case in the bakery's new location, Vickie figured Tim was too busy to check in with her. A week after New Year's and she hadn't heard from him. She'd hoped he'd stop by or at least call to update her on Ken's arrest.

But with Ken safely incarcerated at the county jail, Tim had no reason to come see her. In fact, none of the FBI agents had stopped by. Granted, the bakery was no longer within walking distance of the federal building downtown. It still stung that Tim hadn't come to the grand reopening or made any sort of contact.

Which made her regret for not kissing him much more potent. But in that moment, as she'd realized what he was about to do, a bout of shyness had gripped her. People were watching them, most especially her parents. Not wanting to be a spectacle, she'd shied away from meeting his lips with her own.

Dumb. Why hadn't she just gone with her feelings and not cared what anyone else thought?

Tim must believe she wasn't interested in him.

She couldn't stop thinking about him. She longed to see him. To hear his voice. To spend time with him. Somewhere along the way she'd fallen for the handsome agent. The knowledge had been drilled home the moment he'd come barreling up the staircase after Frodo to rescue her from Ken. Her heart had wept with joy.

But now she was only sad. Sad that she'd missed an opportunity that might not come again.

The bell over the door of the new shop jingled at the arrival of an early morning customer. Pasting on a smile she didn't feel, she lifted her gaze in greeting.

Agent Nina Atkins and a tall, handsome man walked up to the counter. Vickie was glad to see her and had to hold back from immediately asking about Tim. "Hello, Agent Atkins. Welcome to our new location."

"Hello, Vickie." Nina glanced around with approval. "Nice. Bigger than the last place."

"Yes. We are enjoying the space. How are you?"

Nina beamed. "I'm great." She tucked her arm through the man's. "This is US Deputy Marshal Thomas Grant. He just relocated to Billings. Finally."

The man chuckled. "You make it sound like it took a year instead of a few weeks."

"It was a *long* few weeks." Nina glanced up at him with love shining in her eyes.

A stab of jealousy hit Vickie in the chest. She dropped her gaze and wiped at an imaginary speck on the counter. She wanted what they had. To be that in love and unafraid to let anyone see her feelings. "Can I take your order?"

"I'd like two dozen pastries," Nina said. "For our staff meeting."

Vickie's heart clenched. Tim would be there. As she set about the task of loading a pastry box with a variety of sweet treats, she worked up her courage to ask about Tim. "How's Agent Ramsey?"

"He just returned from a visit to his mom's in Florida," Nina replied.

Vickie nearly dropped an apple fritter. Tim had been out of town. Her pulse sped up. Maybe he'd call her now. She finished packing two pink boxes stamped with Petrov Bakery on the top and handed them to Thomas, then took Nina's credit card.

Vickie processed the transaction and handed the card back. "Tell everyone hello for me."

"Of course." Nina stared at her for a moment. "I'm sure Tim will come to see the new place soon."

Vickie bit her lip and darted a glance at Thomas, wishing she and Nina were alone. "That would be nice."

Nina nodded, but didn't move. Instead, she turned to Thomas. "I'll be right out." She gave him a gentle push.

His gaze bounced between the two women and then a light dawned in his eyes. "Ah. Okay. Yes. I'll wait in the car."

Nina motioned for her to follow her to a quiet corner table. When Vickie started straightening the salt and pepper shakers, the agent reached over and placed her hand on hers. "Are you okay? After all you've been through since Christmas…"

Vickie needed someone to confide in. The blond woman sitting across from her seemed so kind and caring. Safe. "I don't know what to do about Tim. Or rather, my feelings for him."

A slow smile spread over the agent's pretty face. "You've fallen for him."

Vickie nodded. "I have."

"Call him," Nina said. "Or better yet, come see him."

"I don't think I could do that," Vickie confessed, as nerves twisted her insides.

"Of course you can," Nina stated with confidence. "You're brave and strong and shouldn't let fear win." She rose. "I better get going."

"Thank you. I'll keep what you've said in mind."

Fear had won too many times throughout Vickie's life.

It was time to be courageous and risk her heart for love.

Tim sat at his desk inside the Tactical K-9 Unit's headquarters doing paperwork. He grabbed the last of the apricot scone he'd snagged to save for an afternoon snack and popped the bite of goodness into his mouth. The tart flavor of the apricot mixed with sugar burst on his tongue.

For a moment he allowed his heart to ache with longing to go to the place where the baked good came from—Petrov Bakery. To see Vickie.

But he was still trying to put her out of his mind and his heart.

He'd managed pretty well while he was out of town, but now that he was back, he kept hoping he'd see her everywhere he went. He'd driven by the new bakery location several times, but forced himself not to stop. It would only be awkward and torturous to see her again.

Then this morning Nina had brought in boxes of treats and told everyone Vickie had said hello. The blanket statement hadn't been directed at him. He'd had to bite his tongue to keep from asking how she was doing. It was none of his business now.

His phone rang. When he answered, one of the dog trainers said, "You're needed in the training center."

Alarm set Tim's heart hammering. Frodo was downstairs in his kennel. Had something happened to him?

He hurried downstairs and skidded to a halt. The center was empty save for Vickie Petrov sitting in the middle of the training center floor.

She looked lovely in jeans and a bright blue sweater that brought out the blue in her eyes. Her blond hair was tied back in a low ponytail and a pink hue brightened her cheeks. A black-masked ball of fawn-colored fluff tumbled over Vickie's outstretched legs.

Tim sat down next to her and held out his fingers for the puppy to sniff. "What's going on here? Who's this?"

"This is Piper. She's a Belgian Malinois," Vickie said, scooping the pup into her hands and depositing her on his lap. "She's a rescue from the animal shelter."

Surprised, he steadied the puppy, his fingers curling into the soft fur. "I didn't know you wanted a pet."

"She's not for me. Though I would like a lapdog one day."

"If she's not yours then…"

"She's a thank-you. To you and the FBI."

He tucked a strand of her blond hair behind her ear. "A thank-you?"

Her eyes held his captive. "If it weren't for you and Frodo, I wouldn't be alive. Ken would have won."

Unable to stop himself, Tim reached for her hand. "I thank God you're safe."

"Me, too." She squeezed his fingers. "I remembered what you told me about your team members bringing in puppies in honor of Agent Morrow."

Tim's breath hitched. "Yes, many of the others have adopted and donated a puppy or a young dog to the K-9 program."

"I'm going to foster her until she's old enough

to be trained as a K-9 officer. The trainers said this breed make great protection dogs." Vickie gave him a shy smile that made his heart thump in his chest. "I'm going to sponsor her in your name."

Stunned by her words, he felt warmth spread through him. "My name?"

She lifted her chin. "You're my hero."

Touched by her words and the gesture, he had to work through the emotions clogging his throat. "That's very generous of you."

The puppy chewed on the zipper of his jacket. He lifted the pup up and stared into her dark eyes. "She's a cutie."

When Vickie didn't respond, he lowered the puppy to the floor between them. "You okay?"

She nodded. "I am. Now." Her mouth kicked up at the corners. "I owe Nina a debt of gratitude."

"How so?"

"When she came by the bakery this morning, she told me I shouldn't let fear win. She's right. I don't want to be afraid anymore. I want to live life to the fullest." Vicki laid a hand on Tim's arm. "You taught me I can be brave even if I don't think I can be."

"You've always been brave, Vickie," he assured her.

A pleased smile touched her lips. "When my parents immigrated from the Ukraine to the United States, they adopted their new Christian church's tradition of Christmas in December. But they didn't want to abandon their family's custom of celebrating the birth of Jesus in January."

"Today?" he guessed.

She nodded. "It's become a holiday for the Ukraine, much like it is here in the US," Vickie explained. "But it has something to do with the difference between the Julian calendar and the Gregorian calendar, both of which date back thousands of years." She shrugged. "Tradition is tradition, as my father would say. Growing up, I loved having two celebrations."

"I would imagine so."

From the front pocket of her jeans, she tugged a sprig of greenery out and held it up for him to see. He sucked in a surprised breath. Mistletoe.

"It's tradition to kiss the one you love beneath the mistletoe."

His pulse leaped. "So I've heard."

She lowered her gaze and fingered the sprig. "I should have let you kiss me."

With the crook of his finger, he lifted her chin. The vulnerability in her eyes made his chest ache. "Are you saying you love me, Vickie?"

"I am."

Elation filled his heart.

"I'd understand if you don't feel the same." Her voice trembled. "We hardly know each other."

He cupped her cheek. "I love you, too."

Her eyes widened. "You do?"

"Yes, I do." His heart swelled with love for this

wondrous woman. He traced his thumb over her lower lip. "I didn't think I'd ever wanted to go down this path again, but you've made me realize how much I was holding back from life. I was too afraid to love again and not be loved in return."

"We were both afraid."

"But not anymore." His voice rang with the conviction filling his soul. "Your heart is safe with me, Vickie."

Delight shone bright in her eyes. "As is your heart with me." She held the mistletoe over his head. "Tradition."

"Who are we to buck tradition?" Yet he refrained from moving, letting her take the lead.

Slowly, she leaned close and pressed her lips to his. He couldn't stop the groan of pleasure from escaping as he slid a hand to the back of her head, deepening the kiss until they were both breathless.

The puppy yipped and pawed at Vickie.

They broke apart with a laugh. The puppy settled in Vickie's lap to gnaw at her fingers before dozing off. A sign the dog trusted her, just as Tim trusted her. He wanted to claim Vickie for his own. To have and to hold. He wanted the whole shebang. A little house, a picket fence and kids. "I have a question for you."

She snuggled the little animal. "Yes?"

He wanted to do this right, make their romance special. Not rush her. He wanted them to have the kind of future he'd only ever dreamed about, but never thought would be possible. "Do you have plans for Valentine's Day?"

A demure smile played on her lush mouth. "Are you asking me for a date?"

He took her hand. "Yes. For this Valentine's Day." He kissed one knuckle. "And the next." He kissed another knuckle. "And the next and the next...." He kissed each knuckle and then turned her palm over to place a kiss in the center.

Delight bubbled in her voice. "Yes!"

He hugged her close. "I was hoping you'd say that."

She pulled back to look into his face, her eyes filled with love. "Merry Christmas."

"Merry Christmas." He dipped his head and kissed her again.

* * * * *

Dear Reader,

I find dogs fascinating and am amazed how canines use their senses to solve crimes. Learning how dogs are used in arson investigations was illuminating. They are considered more accurate than most devices and can cover an entire crime scene in a minimal amount of time compared to human investigators. The bond between dog and handler begins and ends at home. These dogs live with their handlers as one of the family.

I enjoyed giving Frodo and Tim their own story as the final chapter of the Classified K-9 Unit continuity series featuring the men and women of the FBI Tactical K-9 Unit. And pairing the two with the pretty baker, Vickie Petrov, seemed a perfect match. Vickie wasn't too sure she should trust anyone in law enforcement, but the handsome FBI agent and his faithful dog proved trustworthy. Vickie and Tim both had to let go of past wounds to risk opening their hearts to love.

I hope you enjoyed this novella collection. To find the complete Classified K-9 Unit continuity series books, visit the Harlequin Love Inspired Suspense page at www.harlequin.com and click on the miniseries tab. And in 2018 look for the new continuity series featuring military dogs and their handlers.

Until we meet again… God bless,
Terri Reed

Cami Heidegger

Get 2 Free Books,
Plus 2 Free Gifts—
just for trying the Reader Service!

Love Inspired®